Samuel French Acting Edi

A Nice Family Christmas

by Phil Olson

SAMUELFRENCH.COM   SAMUELFRENCH.CO.UK

Copyright © 2017 by Phil Olson
Set Design created by author
All Rights Reserved

A NICE FAMILY CHRISTMAS is fully protected under the copyright laws
of the United States of America, the British Commonwealth, including
Canada, and all other countries of the Copyright Union. All rights,
including professional and amateur stage productions, recitation,
lecturing, public reading, motion picture, radio broadcasting, television
and the rights of translation into foreign languages are strictly reserved.

ISBN 978-0-573-70523-6

www.SamuelFrench.com
www.SamuelFrench.co.uk

FOR PRODUCTION ENQUIRIES

UNITED STATES AND CANADA
Info@SamuelFrench.com
1-866-598-8449

UNITED KINGDOM AND EUROPE
Plays@SamuelFrench.co.uk
020-7255-4302

Each title is subject to availability from Samuel French, depending
upon country of performance. Please be aware that *A NICE FAMILY
CHRISTMAS* may not be licensed by Samuel French in your territory.
Professional and amateur producers should contact the nearest Samuel
French office or licensing partner to verify availability.

CAUTION: Professional and amateur producers are hereby warned that
A NICE FAMILY CHRISTMAS is subject to a licensing fee. Publication of
this play(s) does not imply availability for performance. Both amateurs
and professionals considering a production are strongly advised to apply
to Samuel French before starting rehearsals, advertising, or booking a
theatre. A licensing fee must be paid whether the title(s) is presented for
charity or gain and whether or not admission is charged. Professional/
Stock licensing fees are quoted upon application to Samuel French.

No one shall make any changes in this title(s) for the purpose of
production. No part of this book may be reproduced, stored in a retrieval
system, or transmitted in any form, by any means, now known or yet to
be invented, including mechanical, electronic, photocopying, recording,
videotaping, or otherwise, without the prior written permission of the
publisher. No one shall upload this title(s), or part of this title(s), to any
social media websites.

For all enquiries regarding motion picture, television, and other media
rights, please contact Samuel French.

MUSIC USE NOTE

Licensees are solely responsible for obtaining formal written permission from copyright owners to use copyrighted music in the performance of this play and are strongly cautioned to do so. If no such permission is obtained by the licensee, then the licensee must use only original music that the licensee owns and controls. Licensees are solely responsible and liable for all music clearances and shall indemnify the copyright owners of the play(s) and their licensing agent, Samuel French, against any costs, expenses, losses and liabilities arising from the use of music by licensees. Please contact the appropriate music licensing authority in your territory for the rights to any incidental music.

IMPORTANT BILLING AND CREDIT REQUIREMENTS

If you have obtained performance rights to this title, please refer to your licensing agreement for important billing and credit requirements.

A NICE FAMILY CHRISTMAS was first produced at The Lonny Chapman Group Repertory Theatre in Los Angeles, California, in November 2016. The Artistic Directors were Larry Eisenberg and Chris Winfield, the President was Bert Emmett, the Director was Doug Engalla, the Producer was Alyson York, the Assistant Director was Natalia Santamaria, the set design was by Chris Winfield, the lighting design was by J. Kent Inasy, the Stage Manager/Light Technician was Jordan Hoxsie, the sound design was by Steve Shaw, the Publicist was Nora Feldman, the program was by Alyson York, and the cover art was by Doug Haverty. The cast, in order of appearance, was as follows:

CARL	Greg Barnett
MOM	Belinda Howell
GRANDMA	Marcia Rodd
MICHAEL	Patrick Burke
STACY	Truett Jean Butler
UNCLE BOB	Fox Carney
JILL	Rebekah Dunn

CHARACTERS

CARL – (twenties/thirties) The middle brother. Grew up in the shadow of his older brother, Michael, the doctor. Has a little inferiority complex brought on by Michael. He writes a column for the *Minneapolis Star Tribune* newspaper.

MOM – (fifties/sixties) Very nice. Always putting on a happy face, her goal is to keep the peace and get through the family event without incident. Mom's husband, Carl (senior), died three years ago. She's doing her best to get over the loss and keep everyone happy.

GRANDMA – (seventies/eighties) A real character. Grew up in a one-room house with ten brothers and sisters on a farm in northern North Dakota. Had a very tough life growing up. She is tough as nails, and wants everyone else to be, too.

MICHAEL – (twenties/thirties) The older brother. The doctor. A little nerdy. Wears a bow tie. The favorite son, at least at first. He's a little self-absorbed, a little blind to what he needs to do to keep his marriage to Jill intact.

STACY – (twenties/thirties) The younger sister. Nice. Kind of a wholesome midwestern innocence. Overlooked, but not angry about it.

UNCLE BOB – (fifties/sixties) A partier. Fun-loving. Has an agenda. Everyone has a crazy Uncle Bob.

JILL – (twenties/thirties) Michael's trophy wife. Emotional from being hormonal. Sometimes a little spacey. The only one who understands Grandma's crazy sayings. Wants to make her marriage work with Michael if he can prove he loves her.

SETTING

The living room of Mom's condominium in a suburb of Minneapolis.

TIME

Christmas Eve

ACT I
Early evening

ACT II
Thirty seconds later

ACT I

(The setting is a modest condominium living room complete with a couch, coffee table, and easy chair. Upstage left is a door to the kitchen. Upstage right is a decorated Christmas tree with presents under it, and a box of ornaments. Upstage center is a hallway that leads to the bedroom and bathroom [offstage right], and to a den [offstage left]. There's a dining table covered in a tablecloth stage left near the kitchen. On the dining table is a stack of six plates, six cloth napkins with silverware rolled up in them, and six empty water glasses [not set in their places yet]. Also on the dining table is a plate of Rice Krispies bars. Downstage left is a small bar with liquor bottles and glasses on and behind it. Downstage right is the front door. Next to the door are coat hooks.)

(CARL, wearing a winter coat and carrying a computer bag, knocks, then enters the front door. No one is in the living room.)

CARL. Hello, anyone home? ...Mom, it's me, your favorite son!

(MOM enters from the kitchen.)

MOM. *(Excited.)* Oh, is that you, Michael?

CARL. *(Corrects her.)* No, it's Carl.

MOM. Oh. Well, it's nice to see you, too, dear.

(Excited, looking around.)

Is Michael with ya?!

CARL. No, it's just me.

MOM. Oh. He'll be here, ya know, with his pretty wife.

CARL. Uh-huh. Merry Christmas.

> *(He goes to hug her. It's an arm's-length, pat on the shoulders, awkward hug.)*

MOM. Yeah, Merry Christmas.

CARL. *(Smells something bad.)* Mom, what is that smell?

> *(He looks at the bottom of his shoes to see if he stepped in anything.)*

MOM. Oh, that's the lutefisk.

> *(Pronounced "LEWD-uh-fisk.")*

CARL. *(Not happy.)* Oh, for cryin' in the beer nuts.

> *(He sets down the computer bag by the coffee table and takes off his coat.)*

MOM. You don't like cod fish?

CARL. Well, yeah, but not *dried* cod fish, fermented in *lye.* Who came up with that?

MOM. It's a tradition.

> *(**CARL** hangs up his coat. **GRANDMA** comes out of the hallway.)*

GRANDMA. Who's that out there, is it Michael?

CARL. No, it's Carl.

GRANDMA. Well, we can't all be Michael.

CARL. Good to see you, too, Grandma. I didn't know you were gonna be here.

MOM. I didn't either.

> *(**CARL** goes to hug **GRANDMA**.)*

GRANDMA. Not a hugger.

> *(Holds her hand up. **CARL** stops, steps back.)*

CARL. Okay… So, when did you get in?

MOM. She's been here for three weeks.

GRANDMA. I have not. I got in two days ago.

MOM. Seems like three weeks.

CARL. How's Florida?

GRANDMA. *(Not impressed.)* Florida, huh... God's waiting room.

MOM. Can't beat the weather.

GRANDMA. Too many old people.

MOM. Old age isn't so bad when you consider the alternative.

GRANDMA. Two things happen when ya get old. The first thing is your memory goes.

(They wait for her to say one more. She doesn't.)

CARL. *(After a few beats.)* Is there another one?

GRANDMA. Another what?

CARL. *(To MOM.)* Is she joking?

MOM. I have no idea.

CARL. *(Moving on.)* So, how long are ya stayin'?

GRANDMA. Oh, a month or two.

MOM. Say what, now?

GRANDMA. There's nothin' left for me in Sun City right now. I've been through all the men.

CARL. "Been through all the men"?

MOM. Do not engage.

GRANDMA. I've gotta wait for the new crop to come in. It's pretty high turnover there, ya know. Like Hotel California, you can check in, but ya can't check out... Unless it's on a gurney.

MOM. Lovely.

GRANDMA. If ya know any available men, let me know. I'll go younger.

CARL. I didn't know you were so prolific.

GRANDMA. During the war, I used to swim out to meet the troop ships during Fleet Week.

MOM. No, ya didn't, Grandma.

GRANDMA. I visualized it.

CARL. And you're still active.

MOM. Let's talk about anything else.

GRANDMA. *(Gesturing to her "milk cartons.")* These milk cartons have *not* expired.

MOM. *(Changing the subject. To* **CARL.***)* Can I get you something? We have krum kaka.

> *(Pronounced "kroom kahkah.")*

CARL. Ya know, I think I've had enough "kaka" for today.

GRANDMA. Crumb cake. You need to get back to your roots.

MOM. Would you like some?

CARL. I think I'll just start drinkin'.

> *(He heads to the bar.)*

GRANDMA. Oh, say, would ya take a look at my mole.

> *(Lowers her blouse to* **CARL.***)*

CARL. *(Looking away.)* Oh, no, see, I'm not the doctor. That's Michael. *He's* the doctor.

GRANDMA. Would ya look at it anyway?

CARL. Can I have a few beers, first?

GRANDMA. Your *dad* was a doctor, ya know.

CARL. Yeah, I know.

GRANDMA. That Michael sure is a chip off the old block.

CARL. He's a chip off of *somethin'*.

MOM. Carl is a…

> *(Thinks.)*

What do you do again, dear?

CARL. I'm a writer.

GRANDMA. A waiter?

> *(Laughs.)*

See what I did, there?

CARL. Haven't heard that one before.

> *(***CARL*** gets himself a beer.)*

GRANDMA. Oh, I got a lot of 'em.

CARL. Great. Actually I'm a journalist.

GRANDMA. Ya couldn't get a job as a waiter?

(Laughs, does a verbal "rimshot.")

Ba dump bump. A two-fer. You're welcome.

MOM. Are you still writing for that newspaper?

CARL. The *Star Tribune.*

MOM. How's that goin' for ya?

CARL. Well, newspapers are taking a hit because of the internet, and they've been layin' off people, and I'm afraid I might be next. Which reminds me, I gotta call the office. Sorry about this. It'll just be a minute.

MOM. C'mon, Grandma.

(Gestures to her to go in the kitchen.)

*(**CARL** takes out his cell phone and hits speed dial. **MOM** and **GRANDMA** head to the kitchen.)*

GRANDMA. It's Christmas and he's workin'. Just like Scrooge.

CARL. I'm not Scrooge, Grandma.

GRANDMA. *(As she disappears into the kitchen, skeptical.)* Uh-huh.

CARL. *(Into phone.)* Oh, hey, John, Merry Christmas… Thanks… You called? …Yeah, I'm at my mom's having a nice family Christma–

(He laughs, knowing it's not going to be "nice.")

I'm sorry, I couldn't land it… Sure, what kind of story? …Christmas with my family? Oh, wow, yeah, I don't think anyone's interested in that story… They are? … Well, that's sad… Yeah, I just don't know if they'd be okay with that… Yeah, I know I've been in a dry spell, I just need a good hook…

(Looks toward the kitchen.)

How about old traditions versus the new. I'll see what I can do. Have a good one… Thanks. See ya.

(He hangs up.)

MOM. *(Coming out with a plate of tiny wiener appetizers.)* Who was that?

(She sets the plate on the dining table.)

CARL. My editor.

(He takes out his computer.)

MOM. What did he want?

CARL. Oh, he just wants me to write a story.

(He sits on the couch, puts the computer on the coffee table and opens it.)

MOM. Oh, well, that's nice.

(MICHAEL *knocks, then enters. Wearing a winter coat with a sport coat and bow tie underneath, and nice slacks.)*

MICHAEL. Knock, knock.

MOM. *(Excited, she runs to him.)* It's Michael!

CARL. The boy wonder.

MOM. *(Giving* **MICHAEL** *an awkward, arm's-length hug.)* Merry Christmas.

MICHAEL. Hey, Mom, Merry Christmas.

(He sees **CARL** *on the couch. Indifferent.)*

Carl.

CARL. *(Indifferent.)* Michael.

MICHAEL. *(Indifferent.)* How's it goin'?

CARL. *(Indifferent.)* Good. You?

MICHAEL. *(Indifferent.)* Good.

(After an awkward moment, they realize they have nothing else to say to each other.)

CARL. Okay, then –

MICHAEL. Yeah.

(Taking his coat off, smells something bad.)

Whoa, it smells like burning tires.

MOM. That's the lutefisk.

MICHAEL. *(Not happy.)* Oh, for rice cakes.

GRANDMA. *(Entering.)* Oh, there's Michael. Will you take a look at my mole?

(She lowers her blouse, showing **MICHAEL** *some cleavage.)*

MICHAEL. *(Gags.)* Ohh!

*(**CARL** smiles, then types a few more lines.)*

*(**MICHAEL** composes himself.)*

Hey, Grandma. I didn't know you were gonna be here.

MOM. I didn't either.

GRANDMA. It's your lucky day.

CARL. Where's Jill?

MICHAEL. Oh, she's spending Christmas with her folks.

MOM. I thought she was comin' over here.

MICHAEL. Oh, well, things changed.

(Hangs his coat up.)

GRANDMA. I don't like change.

MOM. That Jill is just the prettiest thing.

(To **MICHAEL.** *)*

How did you ever get her to marry you?

CARL. We all wonder that.

MOM. Not the best cook, though.

MICHAEL. Well, she tries.

MOM. When are you two gonna have a baby?

MICHAEL. We're still working on it, Mom.

MOM. Well, it's so good to see you. I hardly ever do, ya know. I mean you only live twenty minutes away and God forbid you come over more than once a year. I mean, I breast fed ya till you were five!

(To **GRANDMA.** *)*

Those little teeth were sharp!

MICHAEL. Okay, Mom, I'll come by more often.

MOM. Good.

MICHAEL. Things have been a little busy.

>   (**MICHAEL** sees **CARL** typing.)

What's he writing?

>   (He looks over to see.)

CARL. (Closing the computer.) Oh, it's just an assignment for work.

MOM. You still use that little tape recorder when you come up with ideas for your articles?

CARL. Actually, I'm goin' back to using a notepad.

>   (He takes out a small notepad and a pen and shows her.)

MICHAEL. Old school.

MOM. That's nice.

>   (**STACY** opens the front door and enters, wearing a winter coat, shirt, slacks, comfortable shoes, and carrying a purse.)

STACY. Hey everyone.

>   (Everyone ignores her, like she's invisible. She takes her coat off and hangs her purse on a hook. **MOM** starts setting five plates around the dining table.)

GRANDMA. (To **MICHAEL**.) I just adore your wife, what's-her-name.

MICHAEL. Jill.

GRANDMA. No, that's not it... It'll come to me. Anyway, she's like a model, without the throwing up or the crack.

STACY. Merry Christmas.

>   (Hangs her coat up.)

MOM. Carl, when are you gonna get married?

CARL. Oh, gosh, umm, yeah, I don't know.

STACY. Happy New Year.

MICHAEL. How are things with Rita? I thought she might be here.

CARL. Oh, well, she's at her folks'.

GRANDMA. When is your sister comin'?

CARL. She's already here.

GRANDMA. Where?

STACY. I'm right here.

GRANDMA. Oh, yeah. You always were the quiet one.

MICHAEL. It's the "youngest child syndrome."

CARL. Always the doctor.

STACY. *(Going to* **GRANDMA**.*)* It's good to see you, Grandma.

> *(Goes to hug her.)*

GRANDMA. *(Holds her hand up.)* Don't cross the bubble.

STACY. *(Stopping.)* Oh. Okay…

> *(***GRANDMA*** holds her hand out to shake. **STACY** shakes her hand.)*

I love you.

GRANDMA. Whoa, easy! We're not gettin' married.

STACY. Okay.

GRANDMA. Oh, look at you, Stacy, you have gotten so…

> *(Can't think of anything to say.)*

Yes, you have.

STACY. Thanks?

GRANDMA. Never give up.

STACY. *(Uncertain how to take that.)* O-kay.

MOM. *(To* **STACY**.*)* Hi, hon.

STACY. Hi, Mom.

> *(***MOM*** gives **STACY** an awkward, arm's-length hug.)*

MOM. Where's the baby?!

STACY. Oh, she's with the sitter.

GRANDMA. Limit her exposure to her crazy family, right?

STACY. Exactly.

GRANDMA. When do I get to see her?

STACY. Tomorrow morning. She'll be over to open presents.

MOM. She's gotten so big.

GRANDMA. Don't we open presents tonight?

MOM. We're changing things this year.

GRANDMA. Seems like a lot of things are changing around here.

MOM. We might open one or two after dinner.

(**MOM** *starts placing five napkins with silverware rolled up in them by the plates on the dining table.*)

STACY. How are you, Grandma?

GRANDMA. I'm good. Your mom told me you got a divorce.

STACY. She did, did she?

GRANDMA. Did he cheat on ya? Your grandfather never cheated on me. I kept garden shears next to the bed.

(*After a beat, she continues.*)

That's 'cause if he cheated, I would…

(*Motions like she's snipping something with shears.*)

Snip off his hoo hah –

MICHAEL. We got it, we got it.

STACY. Yeah, actually, I *didn't* get a divorce.

GRANDMA. Oh, well, where's your husband?

STACY. (*To* **MOM.**) You didn't tell Grandma?

MOM. I didn't think we'd ever see her again.

STACY. So, she's hearing it for the first time?

MOM. It's all yours. Good luck.

STACY. There's no husband.

GRANDMA. Did he die?

STACY. (*After a beat.*) I'm gay.

GRANDMA. (*Reacts like a cat coughing up a hairball.*) Kah! …Kah! …Kah!

(*Composing herself.*)

But you're so quiet.

STACY. I'm not sure what that has to do with it.

GRANDMA. Well…when did you decide to be gay?

STACY. It's not something you decide.

MICHAEL. It's hereditary, Grandma.

GRANDMA. Hereditary? …Must be from your dad's side.

STACY. That's what *Mom* said.

GRANDMA. Okay, wait, so, how did you have your baby?

STACY. Oh, you know, the usual way.

GRANDMA. With a man?

STACY. No, with a turkey baster.

MICHAEL & CARL. *(Groaning.)* Ohhh.

STACY. Yes, with a man.

GRANDMA. So, you *were* married.

STACY. No, I had the baby before I realized I was gay.

GRANDMA. With some random guy?

STACY. Well, he wasn't *completely* random.

GRANDMA. What a delightful Christmas story.

STACY. We were friends. Still are.

GRANDMA. We didn't have gays when I was growin' up. We had men that liked other men. And it was okay, because they were manly men. Manly men with manly desires for other manly men.

MOM. Okay.

GRANDMA. My how things have changed.

(CARL types a few lines.)

STACY. They really haven't, Grandma.

MOM. Carl, are you gonna be writing the whole night?

CARL. *(Stops typing.)* Sorry, I'll stop.

MOM. *(Changing the subject.)* Anybody want anything?

STACY. We're talkin' about getting married.

GRANDMA. Oh, how wonderful. Who's the lucky guy?

MOM. I have Rice Krispies bars.

STACY. No, see, I'm gay. We just went over that.

MOM. And Christmas cookies.

GRANDMA. Well, who would ya marry, then?

STACY. My partner.

GRANDMA. What's his name?

STACY. No, it's not a he. It's a she.

MOM. I've got a cheese ball.

GRANDMA. So, you'd marry a woman?

STACY. Yeah.

MOM. And crackers.

> (**GRANDMA** *starts to hyperventilate, contorting her face, looking like she's having a seizure.*)

CARL. Are you okay, Grandma?

GRANDMA. Yeah, I just need a minute to process this whole thing. Excuse me.

> (*She calmly goes into the kitchen. From the kitchen.*)

CRAP!

> (*She calmly comes out of the kitchen, smiling.*)

I think I understand, now. So, what's her name?

STACY. LaKeesha.

MOM. (*Holding up the plate of wieners.*) Wieners anyone?

GRANDMA. LaKeesha. That's a pretty name.

> (*Thinks.*)

Is she Swedish?

STACY. No.

GRANDMA. Danish?

STACY. No.

GRANDMA. Finnish?

STACY. No.

GRANDMA. Well, is she a N–

ALL. Grandma!

GRANDMA. Norwegian?

STACY. No.

*(**MOM** whispers into **GRANDMA**'s ear.)*

Why is she whispering?

GRANDMA. *(Re: What **MOM** told her. Calmly.)* Oh, I see... One second.

(She goes into the kitchen.)

MOTHER F–

ALL. GRANDMA!

*(**GRANDMA** calmly comes out of the kitchen.)*

GRANDMA. *(Smiling.)* I'm very happy for you.

STACY. Thank you.

GRANDMA. Is she Lutheran?

STACY. Catholic.

GRANDMA. *(Like she's coughing up a hairball, puts her right hand over her heart like it's a heart attack, bends over.)* Kah! ...Kah! ...Kah!

CARL. She's havin' a stroke.

MICHAEL. Stay with us, Grandma.

(Checking her pulse.)

STACY. Come to the light, Grandma. Follow my voice.

MOM. I'll get you some water, Grandma.

(She goes to the bar.)

CARL. It's interesting that "Catholic" would set her off.

MICHAEL. Are you okay, Grandma? You seem a little off.

MOM. Have you been snorting Metamucil again?

GRANDMA. Don't judge me.

MICHAEL. Your pulse is a little high.

CARL. Ya think?

GRANDMA. I miss the days when our only concern was Nazis.

STACY. It was a simpler time.

> (**STACY** *goes behind the bar and pours herself a glass of wine.*)

MOM. *(Handing* **GRANDMA** *the water.)* Here you go.

GRANDMA. Thanks. Ya know, I'm actually a very accepting person.

MOM. Well…

GRANDMA. Oh, yeah. When I was with Martin Luther King…

STACY. You marched with Martin Luther King?!

GRANDMA. Oh, I didn't *march* with him.

MOM. Okay.

CARL. *(To* **STACY.***)* Have ya set a date?

STACY. For the wedding? No, we still have a few things to work out.

CARL. Like what?

STACY. Why do you wanna know, nosy?

CARL. Just curious.

STACY. She doesn't get along very well with her father. He's not very understanding.

MOM. Al?

STACY. You know him?

MOM. I sat next to Al and Roberta at the club on Thanksgiving. They're very nice.

STACY. What did you talk about?

MOM. Golf.

GRANDMA. Your mom was a great golfer, ya know. Still is. She won twenty-one club championships.

STACY. I know. She's a great competitor.

> (**UNCLE BOB** *knocks on the door.*)

MOM. Now, who could that be?

> (**CARL** *opens it.* **UNCLE BOB** *comes in carrying a fifth of whiskey, wearing a Santa hat and winter coat. He's slightly tipsy, not drunk.*)

UNCLE BOB. Hey, everyone. Merry Christmas!

MICHAEL. And *now* it's a party.

CARL. Uncle Bob. I didn't know you were gonna be here.

MOM. I didn't either.

CARL. And look. You brought…

> *(Taken aback.)*

A bottle of whiskey.

UNCLE BOB. Well, ya can't spell "B.Y.O.B." without "Bob."

> *(He laughs.)*

Am I right? Huh, huh?

CARL. Unfortunately.

UNCLE BOB. *(Holding out the bottle.)* Hey, you want a toot? A little snortski?

CARL. No, thanks.

UNCLE BOB. Christmas is the one time of year when alcoholics go unnoticed.

> *(He laughs.)*

Pound it.

> *(Holds his fist out to CARL, who doesn't "pound it.")*

No? Okay.

CARL. How did ya get here?

UNCLE BOB. Oh, I took the Yoober.

> *(Sees MOM.)*

Hey, Helen, good to see ya. Thanks for inviting me.

MOM. I didn't know I did.

UNCLE BOB. It was at Carl's funeral.

> *(He looks at CARL.)*

Your dad.

CARL. Uh-huh.

UNCLE BOB. *(To MOM.)* You said, "Stop by any time."

MOM. That was three years ago.

UNCLE BOB. I knew it. I should have called. Tomorrow I will. Unless I'm stayin' over.

(Smells something.)

Hey, I didn't know you had a sewage treatment plant nearby.

MOM. That's the lutefisk.

UNCLE BOB. *(Gagging.)* Oh, mylanta! ...Good thing I brought my beef jerky.

MICHAEL. You brought beef jerky?

UNCLE BOB. Always be prepared.

MICHAEL. For what?

UNCLE BOB. For the giant asteroid that's heading toward Earth that the government doesn't want us to know about.

MICHAEL. I think that was just a movie.

UNCLE BOB. Or *was* it?

(CARL jots down something in his notepad.)

STACY. *(Ignoring his craziness.)* Hi, Uncle Bob.

UNCLE BOB. Oh, my gosh, it's Stacy. How are you?

GRANDMA. She's gay.

UNCLE BOB. Good for you.

GRANDMA. She got it from her dad.

UNCLE BOB. I knew it. He used to look at me askance.

MICHAEL. Like I'm looking at you right now?

UNCLE BOB. You, too? Hey, that's okay, Michael. No judgments here. We're all a little bit gay, aren't we?

GRANDMA. I'm not.

UNCLE BOB. Hey, Stacy, do you know Robert Hansen?

STACY. No. Why?

UNCLE BOB. I used to work with him. *He's* a gay.

STACY. We don't all know each other.

MOM. How did you know what time to be here?

UNCLE BOB. You mentioned it on the Facebook.

MOM. Oh, I didn't know everybody could see that.

MICHAEL. Yeah, Mom. The whole world.

MOM. Oh, well, take off your coat and make yourself at home.

CARL. *(Under his breath.)* Oh, great.

UNCLE BOB. Hey, why does Santa Claus go down the chimney Christmas Eve? ...Because it soots him.

(He laughs while taking off his coat.)

GRANDMA. I don't get it.

CARL. This is gonna be a long night.

MOM. Bob, have you met my mother, Clara. She came up from Florida.

UNCLE BOB. *(Hangs up his coat.)* Oh, I didn't know your mother was still alive.

GRANDMA. "Still alive"? I'm gonna be dancin' on *your* grave, Clown Boy.

UNCLE BOB. Well, it's nice that you could spend the holidays in Minnesota in the snow where it's more Christmasy.

GRANDMA. Jesus was born in a desert. If I wanted "Christmasy," surrounded by heat, sand and Jewish people, I would have stayed in Florida.

MOM. *(Ignoring* **GRANDMA.***)* I haven't seen you in awhile. How are your kids?

*(***MOM*** sets out a sixth plate and a napkin with silverware rolled in it on the dining table.)*

UNCLE BOB. Well, my son is in Omaha with his wife and children.

GRANDMA. Is that the embezzler?

UNCLE BOB. Well, he did get in a little trouble but it was all a misunderstanding.

GRANDMA. So was Pearl Harbor.

UNCLE BOB. My daughter is in Burnsville right now.

GRANDMA. The stripper?

UNCLE BOB. Actually, she's a cheerleader for the Vikings.

GRANDMA. Same thing.

UNCLE BOB. So, Helen, I know I haven't seen you since the funeral, and I just wanna say again how sorry I am about Carl…

    (Looks at **CARL**.*)*

Carl senior.

CARL. Uh-huh.

UNCLE BOB. He was a good brother to me and I'm sure a good husband to you.

MOM. Thanks.

UNCLE BOB. So, how are ya doin'? Are ya doin' okay?

MOM. Yeah, I'm fine.

UNCLE BOB. I like your condo.

GRANDMA. It's too small.

MOM. Well, I didn't need all the room in the old house since it's just me, so, here I am.

UNCLE BOB. Yeah, it's nice. So, what else is goin' on? What about you, Carl? What are you doin' these days? Are you datin' anyone?

MOM. He's dating Rita.

MICHAEL. You've been going out for a few years, now, haven't ya.

CARL. Actually, we're kind of on hiatus.

MOM. Oh, what happened?

MICHAEL. Did ya screw it up? I bet ya screwed it up.

    (To **MOM**.*)*

He screwed it up.

CARL. I didn't screw it up. It was just…somethin' I said.

GRANDMA. Did ya call her a "floozy"? …Women don't like that. I never did. Well, sometimes…

    (Looks up, remembering.)

And then he would take me over his knee, and spanky, spanky, spanky –

MOM. Okay. Carl, you were saying?

CARL. Oh, well, actually, it's a little personal.

GRANDMA. There are no secrets in this family. Except when I flew those spy missions with Charles Lindbergh.

MOM. No, ya didn't.

GRANDMA. That's when he introduced me to the Mile High Club.

CARL, MICHAEL, STACY & MOM. *(Groaning.)* Ohhh.

MOM. You were saying, Carl?

CARL. Oh, boy. Alright, I guess it might help my story.

STACY. Your what?

CARL. Oh, nothin'. So, the last time I went out with Rita, she asked me where our relationship was going.

UNCLE BOB. Ouch.

MOM. What did you say?

CARL. I said it was going to the Olive Garden and then to a movie.

MOM. Oh, no.

STACY. No kidding.

CARL. If I just thought before opening my mouth we might still be together, but nooooo.

GRANDMA. If "ifs" and "buts" were candy and nuts, every day would be Christmas.

CARL. I don't get it. We had a great thing going. We had fun together, we had a lot of stuff in common. I don't know what happened?

STACY. Ya really don't?

CARL. No.

STACY. You've been going out for two years. At your age ya can't expect a woman to do that forever.

MICHAEL. They have an expiration date.

CARL. They what?

MICHAEL. You know, their…

(Motions to his lower area.)

Lady parts.

STACY. Is that the medical term for it?

MICHAEL. Women want children, okay. If you're not gonna be the one to make that happen, they need to move on before, you know…

(Motions to his lower area.)

Dust bowl.

GRANDMA. I have a dust bowl… I keep plastic fruit in it.

MICHAEL. Women have a plan. They don't just meander through life, like you. They want a ring. A big one. Which means you need to make more money, and get a better job.

CARL. I have a good job.

MICHAEL. Writing a gossip column?

CARL. It's not a gossip column, it's a "human interest" column.

UNCLE BOB. Ya want my advice?

CARL. Oh, wow, umm –

UNCLE BOB. Don't worry, I'm qualified, okay, 'cause I was married once before, in the eighties. Then another two times in the nineties. So, I'm pretty much an expert.

CARL. Apparently.

UNCLE BOB. Tell her what she wants to hear. It's easier. Ya won't fight as much. Then, if things go off the rails, ya just move out in the middle of the night. No forwarding address. Change your phone number, too. At first it's tough on the kids, but eventually they forget ya.

CARL. Is that what *you* did?

UNCLE BOB. Yes, it is.

CARL. How did that work out for ya?

UNCLE BOB. Not well at all.

MOM. Your son still not talkin' to you?

UNCLE BOB. Not for a couple years.

MOM. What goes around, comes around.

GRANDMA. That's my nickname in Sun City.

MOM. *(Re:* **GRANDMA.***)* So proud of you.

STACY. *(To* **UNCLE BOB.***)* You should call your son.

UNCLE BOB. Oh, he doesn't wanna talk to me.

GRANDMA. Well, we can't solve everything. Now, let's get back to Carl and Rita.

CARL. Oh, great.

GRANDMA. Carl, honey, I'd like to tell you a story about another little girl, just like you.

> *(***CARL*** reacts to "just like you.")*

She was full of hope and promise, too. As fortune would have it, that little girl met a little boy. We'll call him…"Magic Mike." They quickly fell in love and did things that kids do, ya know, ice fishing with dynamite, bootlegging. Then one day that little girl left Magic Mike. She just couldn't commit to one man. So she committed to the U.S. Navy. Until they ran out of penicillin… You get what I'm tryin' to tell ya?

CARL. No.

GRANDMA. You need to jump ship and swim back to Rita before your dingy turns green.

MICHAEL. Grandma's right.

CARL. She is?!

MICHAEL. Yeah, you should go back to her.

CARL. I don't know if I can do that.

STACY. Baby.

> *(***GRANDMA*** sniffs **CARL.***)*

CARL. What are you doin'?

GRANDMA. I think your diaper needs changing.

MOM. *(Changing the subject.)* Okay, this might be a good time to make an announcement.

GRANDMA. *(Making an announcement.)* Cheez Whiz does *not* contain "whiz."

MOM. *(After a beat, she ignores* **GRANDMA**.*)* If everyone is good this Christmas, I'll give all of you a big surprise.

GRANDMA. Okay, when you say "good this Christmas," how long are we talkin', like an hour? 'Cause that's my limit.

MOM. If everyone is good tonight, starting right now, and ending at midnight, I'll give everyone a big present.

UNCLE BOB. Am I part of this?

MOM. Sure.

GRANDMA. What are the ground rules?

MOM. You have to be good.

UNCLE BOB. Can ya be more specific? 'Cause some people's idea of good is different than others.

GRANDMA. Last Halloween in Sun City I dressed up like Eve, ya know, in the Garden of Eden, and all I wore were three oak leaves…

> *(Motions with her hand where the oak leaves were placed.)*

Until a stiff breeze came up, and "whoosh" off they went.

MICHAEL. That's disturbing.

UNCLE BOB. Do ya have any pictures?

STACY. So many things wrong with that.

MOM. Is there a point, Grandma?

GRANDMA. The point is, I was bad. But that was actually good, according to the Sun City Nudist Club.

MOM, STACY, CARL & MICHAEL. *(Groaning.)* Ohh.

GRANDMA. Hot yoga every Tuesday.

> *(She bends over.)*

MOM, STACY, CARL & MICHAEL. *(Groaning.)* OHHH!

UNCLE BOB. Is there a sign-up sheet?

MOM. Okay, back to the contest. I'll be more specific. You have to do something unselfish for someone that you care for.

GRANDMA. Pass.

MOM. You can't pass.

MICHAEL. Why the contest, Mom?

MOM. Oh, I don't know, honey. Life is short. We need to seize the day, and do something nice for those we care for.

UNCLE BOB. Okay, what do we win? What's the prize?

MOM. Something great. And there will be a grand prize for the best unselfish deed.

UNCLE BOB. I'm in.

STACY. Me, too.

MICHAEL. Me, too.

CARL. Me, too.

GRANDMA. Can ya put a monetary value on the prize? I don't do unselfish deeds for free.

MOM. It's priceless.

GRANDMA. I don't know. It's a lot of pressure. I mean, I have no control over what I'm gonna say. Or my bladder.

STACY. C'mon, Grandma, you gotta be in on this.

GRANDMA. Can I get a handicap? Like, let me do five inappropriate things.

MOM. You've already done five inappropriate things.

GRANDMA. Okay, fine, I'm in. I just need tequila and a Xanax.

MOM. That's six.

STACY. Ya need any help in the kitchen, Mom?

MOM. Sure.

GRANDMA. You stay, I'll help her. I need to check on the lutefisk.

EVERYONE. *(Groaning.)* Ohh.

UNCLE BOB. Can I help?

MOM. *(Surprised he asked.)* Oh, umm...sure.

GRANDMA. He's tryin' to score points for the contest.

>   (**GRANDMA**, **MOM**, *and* **UNCLE BOB** *go into the kitchen.*)

STACY. Okay, be honest. What do you guys think about me getting married?

CARL. I think the minute ya marry someone, you've established a motive for murder.

STACY. Very helpful. Michael?

MICHAEL. Well, in all fairness, marriage can be really hard work, okay, and a lot of the time you'll be discouraged and let down and ignored, and you just want to leave and never come back, and sometimes you wanna kill your spouse but you don't because they have laws.

STACY. *(Waiting for more. After a few beats.)* Well, that was inspirational. Carl, any other pearls of wisdom?

CARL. I think if you wanna get married, that's fine. My only question is, why would you ever wanna get married? Seriously.

STACY. It's legal.

CARL. I know. And that's another thing. Why would you ever want it to be legal? Do you have any idea how great you had it when it wasn't legal? I'm hoping some day they outlaw heterosexual marriage. If they did that, I'd still be in a relationship today. "Hey, honey, I'd love to marry you, but you know what, it's not legal. I'm really sorry but my hands are tied. I wish I could do something, I really do, but I can't. It's the law. Now, let's go to the Olive Garden."

>   (**GRANDMA** *enters, carrying salt and pepper shakers. She sets them on the dining table.*)

MICHAEL. You're never gonna find anyone as good as Rita.

CARL. I was thinkin' the same thing about you and Jill.

STACY. *(To* **CARL**.*)* Why don't you and Rita live with each other for awhile. Kind of a trial run.

>   (**UNCLE BOB** *enters.*)

GRANDMA. We never "lived with each other" when I was your age. It was all or nothin'. You kids with your "living in sin." It's like Sodom and Gomorrah these days, with your "sexting" and your "twerking." I got your twerking right here.

(She twerks.)

Here ya go. Here's your twerking. Badonka donk. How do ya like that? Huh? Huh? Break it down, break it down, feed the chicken, pop and lock, shake and bake, now, we're talkin'.

(One final butt thrust.)

Bam!

(She stops.)

CARL. I will never un-see that.

MICHAEL. I'm scarred for life.

UNCLE BOB. *(Pulls out a dollar bill, holding it out.)* Will you do that again?

MICHAEL. You know what, Carl, Rita might not be the one for you. Face it, you may not be able to work out your differences.

CARL. Yeah, whatever. It's not like you and Jill haven't had your problems.

MICHAEL. Why? What did you hear?

CARL. *(Suspicious.)* Nothing. Is there something you'd like to tell me?

MICHAEL. No. Stacy, did Mom say she had cheese and crackers?

STACY. Uh-huh.

(She doesn't move.)

MICHAEL. Could you get it for us, please?

STACY. Sure.

(As she goes into the kitchen.)

Hey, Mom, I'm doin' somethin' unselfish for someone I care f–

(Gags.)

STACY. Oh, jeez, I can't even say it.

> (**MICHAEL** *looks at* **UNCLE BOB**, *trying to hint for him to leave.*)

UNCLE BOB. Oh, you want privacy. I'll just...check my email.

> *(He exits to the den.)*

> (**MICHAEL** *looks at* **GRANDMA** *with the same hint.*)

GRANDMA. Oh, for spankin' the neighbor's baby, we just left.

> *(As she exits to the kitchen.)*

You're like the Bobbsey twins with your little girly secrets. Put some lipstick on each other and play pattycake.

> *(Disappears into the kitchen.)*

CARL. *(Suspicious.)* So...how's Jill?

MICHAEL. She's fine. She went back to work, teaching.

CARL. Why isn't she here?

MICHAEL. Well, I invited her.

CARL. You "invited her"?

MICHAEL. I hope she'll be here, but...

CARL. Where is she?

MICHAEL. I assume she's at her parents', but, I don't know.

CARL. You don't know?

MICHAEL. I'm gonna go over there later. Hopefully, she'll be there.

CARL. Did you have an argument?

MICHAEL. We're separated.

CARL. Whoa.

> *(He puts his hand on* **MICHAEL**'s *shoulder like he's going to console him, then.)*

So...she's available?

MICHAEL. What?!

CARL. *(Backing away.)* No, no, of course, you're still married.

MICHAEL. I knew it. You still have a thing for Jill.

CARL. I don't have a thing for Jill.

MICHAEL. You hugged her. I saw it. And you don't hug people without intent.

CARL. It was a hug. You should try it. Okay, so, what happened? When did you and Jill separate?

MICHAEL. Three weeks ago.

CARL. Okay, hold on a second. You're giving me crap for Rita leaving me at the same time that Jill left you?

MICHAEL. I never said she left me. Maybe I left her.

CARL. Did you leave her?

MICHAEL. *(Cries.)* Nooo.

CARL. I'm surprised it took this long.

MICHAEL. Why would you say that?

CARL. I just figured she was with you for your money.

MICHAEL. You think she was with me for my money?

CARL. Well, why else would she be with you? I mean, come on.

*(He gestures to **MICHAEL**.)*

MICHAEL. I have good qualities.

CARL. Yeah, sure, you do. Okay, so, what happened?

MICHAEL. Well, when I got back from rehab, things were –

CARL. *(Interrupting him.)* Whoa, whoa, whoa, you went to rehab?

MICHAEL. Yeah.

CARL. Like "Betty Ford" rehab?

MICHAEL. Hazelden. I thought you knew.

CARL. No. When?

MICHAEL. The first time or the second time?

CARL. You went there twice?!

MICHAEL. I thought you knew.

CARL. Why would I know that? You never told me.

MICHAEL. Well, if we talked more than once a year.

CARL. Why would we do *that?*

MICHAEL. I was there for a month both times. Charlie Sheen was there. I'm not supposed to tell you that.

CARL. What were you in for? Is that how you say it, or is that for prison?

MICHAEL. Mostly alcohol.

CARL. "Mostly"? Oh, jeez, I don't even wanna know.

MICHAEL. Thanks for the support.

CARL. How did it get to this?

MICHAEL. I don't know, the pressure of not having a baby, the fear of losing Jill, pressure at work, take your pick.

CARL. You can't go to rehab.

MICHAEL. Why not?

CARL. You're my older brother. You're supposed to be the squared away one.

MICHAEL. I couldn't help it. It's a disease.

CARL. Cancer is a disease.

MICHAEL. Look, I'm fine now.

CARL. You know what kind of pressure this puts on me to be the responsible one? I don't wanna be responsible. I don't wanna have to step up to the plate. I like being second most squared away. I'm comfortable with it. There's no pressure.

MICHAEL. "Second most squared away"? I think you just gave yourself a promotion.

CARL. You mean I'm third?

MICHAEL. Yeah, I would put Stacy way above you in squared-awayness.

CARL. Dangit.

MICHAEL. Well, yeah. And it's about time you were responsible.

CARL. Okay, first of all, "He who throws stones in glass houses...*don't.*" Second, I'm not ready for responsibility.

MICHAEL. Are you happy?

CARL. Oh, for crap sake.

MICHAEL. Seriously, are you happy?

CARL. Well, yeah, I mean, not *now*.

MICHAEL. When are you happy?

CARL. Well...when I write an article that people like.

MICHAEL. Any other time?

CARL. Alright, when I'm with Rita, okay. I'm happy then. Is that what you wanted to hear?

MICHAEL. Yeah. Good for you, you figured it out. Happiness is not real unless it's shared.

CARL. Says the guy who's separated from his wife.

MICHAEL. She left me for no reason.

CARL. 'Cause you're a jerk.

MICHAEL. Not helping.

CARL. Ya know, we're kinda in the same boat, okay.

MICHAEL. *(Emotional.)* I can't lose Jill. She makes me wanna be human.

CARL. Well, it's good that you can dream.

MICHAEL. *(Holding back tears.)* If I lose Jill, I will fall into the dark abyss, and I will never come out.

> *(He cries.)*

CARL. See? There *is* a bright side.

> *(**MOM**, **GRANDMA**, *and* **STACY** *come out of the kitchen.* **STACY** *is carrying a plate with a cheese ball and crackers. She sets it on the coffee table.)*

MICHAEL. *(Whispers to **CARL**.)* Don't tell anyone about Jill.

MOM. Is everyone okay out here?

CARL. Jill left Michael.

MOM. Oh, no.

MICHAEL. Thanks.

CARL. And he was in rehab.

STACY. What?

MOM. Well, I knew that.

(**MOM** *starts placing the water glasses around the six plates on the dining table.*)

GRANDMA. We didn't have alcoholics when I was growin' up. We had men that could drink a bottle of Scotch, drive to work, fly an airplane, fool around with the stewardess, come home to a loving wife, and beat the kids to sleep... Those were the days.

(**CARL** *writes something in his notepad.* **STACY** *sees him.*)

STACY. What are ya writin' there, Carl?

CARL. Oh, just somethin' for work.

STACY. *(To* **MICHAEL**.*)* Why don't you and Jill try couples therapy.

MICHAEL. Oh, no.

MOM. There's no shame in that.

GRANDMA. We didn't have couples therapy when I was your age. We solved our marital problems with an open and honest conversation followed by a duel.

STACY. Well, things are different now, Grandma.

GRANDMA. *(To* **MICHAEL**.*)* I'll give ya therapy. Whatever you're doin' wrong, stop it. Just stop it. There, I just saved ya five thousand bucks.

MICHAEL. Thanks.

GRANDMA. Is Stacy the only one in the room with a functional relationship?

MOM. And she's the only one with a child.

GRANDMA. And she doesn't have commitment issues.

CARL. And she's not an alcoholic.

MICHAEL. Okay, okay, I get it. Stacy wins.

MOM. *(To* **STACY**.*)* So, what's your secret, hon?

STACY. Oh, umm...good communication?

MICHAEL. Oh, jeez!

CARL. Here we go.

STACY. Well, ya gotta communicate and share your feelings.

MICHAEL. Oh, for shavin' the dog's butt.

GRANDMA. What happened to the good old days when men held in their feelings until their hearts exploded.

> (**UNCLE BOB** *comes out of the den wearing the Santa hat with a big mistletoe pinned to the top of it.*)

MOM. What's that on your head?

UNCLE BOB. It's mistletoe.

> (*Holding his arms out for a kiss.*)

MOM. Take it off.

UNCLE BOB. Oh, come on, just one little kiss?

MOM. You're embarrassing yourself, now take it off.

UNCLE BOB. Oh, alright.

> (*He takes off the hat and looks around for a place to put it. He doesn't see a place, so he stuffs it in the front of his pants, the mistletoe hanging over his crotch, unaware of how ridiculous it looks. Everyone stares at it. After a few beats.*)

MOM. You need counseling.

> (*She yanks the hat out of his pants and puts it behind the bar.*)

> (**JILL** *knocks on the door.*)

Now, who could that be?

> (**MICHAEL** *answers the door.* **JILL** *has a tote bag over her shoulder and is wearing a dress under a winter coat.*)

JILL. Merry Christmas.

MICHAEL. You're here.

JILL. Hi.

MOM. It's Jill!

JILL. Hi, Helen.

> (*Sets her tote bag down under the coat hooks.*)

MOM. Look at you, you're so pretty.

(Gives JILL *an arm's-length, uncomfortable hug.)*

JILL. Oh, well, it's the moisturizer.

GRANDMA. We didn't have fancy moisturizer when I was
your age. We rubbed goat jam on our face.

JILL. *(Pronounced "you.")* Ewe.

GRANDMA. No, "goat."

CARL. Hi, Jill.

(He hugs her for MICHAEL's *benefit.)*

JILL. *(Hugging him back.)* Hi, Carl.

CARL. *(Still hugging her, looking at* MICHAEL, *rubbing it in.)*
You look good.

JILL. *(Still hugging him back.)* So do you.

CARL. *(Still hugging her while looking at* MICHAEL.) Oh, yeah.

MICHAEL. Okay, okay, that's enough.

(He separates them.)

*(*JILL *takes out a little gift bag with cookies in it
from her tote bag.)*

JILL. *(Handing the gift bag of cookies to* MOM.) I brought
cookies.

MOM. Oh, how nice. Did you make 'em?

JILL. All by myself. Try one.

MOM. *(Not a fan of* JILL's *cooking.)* Oh, okay.

(She takes out a cookie and takes a tiny bite as JILL
watches. It's horrible.)

Yum.

JILL. *(Smiles.)* Thanks.

*(*JILL *turns away to hang up her coat.* MOM *gags,
then puts the rest of the cookie back in the bag.)*

MOM. Let's just find a place for these, then.

(She puts the gift bag by the Christmas tree.)

CARL. *(To* JILL.) I thought you were at your parents'.

JILL. I was. I wanted to come over and say hi.

(She cries a little.)

Ohh.

(Composes herself.)

I'm sorry.

GRANDMA. What the hell is wrong with her?

STACY. She's taking fertility hormones. They make her emotional.

JILL. No, I'm not on those anymore.

(Holding in tears.)

GRANDMA. What, do you just like to cry, then?

MOM. Grandma, be nice.

GRANDMA. What are we, Baptists?

MICHAEL. It's the hormones. They're still in her system.

JILL. It's the holidays. I get emotional. I'm sorry. I haven't been myself.

UNCLE BOB. Don't be sorry. Christmas is like an emotional roller coaster flying off the track, past the Tunnel of Love and into the House of Broken Dreams. And then into the petting zoo.

(Imitating a sheep.)

Baaaah.

JILL. *(Emotional.)* That's what *I* was thinking.

STACY. *(Re: **UNCLE BOB**'s description.)* That was very specific.

MICHAEL. *(To **JILL**.)* You remember Uncle Bob.

JILL. Hi.

UNCLE BOB. Merry Christmas.

MOM. And you know my mother, Clara.

JILL. Oh, hi, I thought you were…

GRANDMA. Dead? Yeah, I get that a lot.

JILL. I was gonna say, "in Florida."

GRANDMA. Same thing.

CARL. *(To **JILL**.)* I heard you left Michael.

MICHAEL. Thanks again.

JILL. *(Emotional.)* It's been a tough three months.

CARL. Three months?!

> *(To MICHAEL.)*

You said three weeks.

MICHAEL. I did? I meant three months.

MOM. You haven't seen each other for three months?

GRANDMA. When your grandfather was in the army, I didn't see him for two years. I tell ya, when he got home, I was on him like a baboon on a banana.

MOM. Ya know what, I bet you two wanna have a little privacy since you haven't seen each other for so long.

STACY. Why don't we go in the kitchen so they can talk.

GRANDMA. Again with the goin' in the kitchen?

MOM. C'mon, let's stuff the turkey.

> *(Heads for the kitchen.)*

GRANDMA. *(Following MOM.)* That's a pose in hot nude yoga.

CARL, MICHAEL & STACY. *(Groaning.)* Ohhh.

MOM. Here we go.

> *(MOM, GRANDMA, and STACY disappear into the kitchen. UNCLE BOB goes in the den. CARL stays.)*

You comin', Carl?

CARL. Sure. Because it's the unselfish thing to do.

> *(He exits to the kitchen.)*

STACY. Brown nose.

> *(Disappears into the kitchen.)*

> *(MICHAEL and JILL are alone.)*

JILL. So…how is everything?

> *(Whimpers.)*

Ohh.

> *(Collects herself.)*

I'm okay, I'm okay.

MICHAEL. Are ya sure?

JILL. *(Holding back the tears.)* Yeah.

MICHAEL. So…what have you been doing the last three months?

JILL. Well, I've been at my parents'.

MICHAEL. So, you came back to…apologize?

JILL. What?!

MICHAEL. Okay, so that's a "no." No problem. So…do you wanna come back?

JILL. Why should I?

MICHAEL. Because…we're married?

JILL. You don't care about me.

MICHAEL. I do, too.

JILL. Prove it.

MICHAEL. Okay, fine… Could you first just tell me what I did to make you leave?

JILL. You don't know?

MICHAEL. No.

JILL. You spent ten thousand dollars on commemorative plates.

MICHAEL. It's about the money?

> (**CARL** *bursts out of the kitchen, followed by* **MOM**, **GRANDMA**, *and* **STACY**. **MOM** *is carrying a seventh plate, napkin, and silverware for* **JILL**.)

CARL. You spent ten thousand dollars on commemorative plates?!

MICHAEL. Can anyone have a private moment around here?!

CARL. No. What kind of plates are they?

JILL. You know, *The Wizard of Oz, Star Trek*, Elvis Presley.

GRANDMA. Elvis Presley was not a good kisser.

STACY. You were with Elvis –

MOM. Don't.

GRANDMA. Your grandfather, now he was a good kisser. He kissed like he was snakin' a drain.

MOM. Grandma.

GRANDMA. He could breathe through his ears.

EVERYONE. GRANDMA!

CARL. *(Typing on the computer.)* I didn't think anyone actually bought those plates.

>   *(**UNCLE BOB** enters from the den, taking a swig of whiskey from his bottle.)*

MOM. Carl, are you still writing?

>   *(**MOM** sets the plate and napkin with silverware for **JILL**'s place.)*

CARL. Sorry, I'll wait 'til later.

>   *(He stops typing, leaves the computer open, and takes out the notepad and pen.)*

MICHAEL. *(Defensive.)* A lot of people buy those plates. They're a collector's item, and an investment.

STACY. Not sure I would call 'em an investment.

JILL. He's obsessive compulsive. I just couldn't take his OCD.

MICHAEL. I'm not OCD.

STACY. It's more like a multiple addictive disorder.

MICHAEL. Right. Wait, no. It's not multiple, it's just three or four.

JILL. I mean, I thought all of that was over after his two stints in rehab.

UNCLE BOB. You went to rehab twice?! …So did I. Up top.

>   *(Holds his hand up for a "high five" from **MICHAEL**. He doesn't get the high five.)*

MICHAEL. You were in rehab and you're drinking?

UNCLE BOB. I can stop at any time.

>   *(To **JILL**.)*

Continue with your plate story.

JILL. When he bought the plates, that was the last straw. He didn't change, he was the same person, and…I just needed a break.

MICHAEL. But I only needed the limited edition *Star Trek* Captain series to complete the set.

>   *(To* CARL.*)*

They only made, like, five of 'em.

>   *(To* JILL.*)*

Then I was done.

JILL. Is that true?

GRANDMA. Or is it the booze talking?

MICHAEL. I've been sober for five months.

MOM. Good for you, Michael.

>   *(*MOM *sets the water glasses around the table.)*

CARL. He never acted that way when we were growing up. I mean, he was a jerk, but –

MOM. *(Trying to cheer up the conversation.)* Christmas time, yaay, we have a contest, do something nice for somebody! Yaay!

JILL. *(To* CARL.*)* I don't know. Maybe it's the pressure of not being able to have kids. I mean, all our friends have kids. We're the only ones that don't. Maybe he was overcompensating.

STACY. *(To* JILL.*)* With plates?

MICHAEL. Feel free to direct the conversation to me.

GRANDMA. *(To* MICHAEL.*)* You just need to pull your head outta your butt and knock off that stupid plate business.

MICHAEL. Grandma, I'm just a little sensitive right now.

GRANDMA. Oh, honey, did I offend you?

MICHAEL. A little.

GRANDMA. Oh, I'm sorry. I didn't mean to hurt you. I mean, it's just words. It's not like getting hit by a howitzer on Normandy Beach on D-Day. It's just words, so why don't you suck it up, ya marshmallow.

MICHAEL. That went from an apology to an assault.

GRANDMA. Walk it off.

MICHAEL. I feel like I'm at boot camp.

UNCLE BOB. I'm gettin' a little excited, here.

MOM. Contest! Who's gonna win?!

GRANDMA. *(To* **MICHAEL.***)* What are you, one of those people who wakes up every mornin', lookin' for somethin' to be offended by?

MICHAEL. No.

GRANDMA. Good. So, other than the plate business, are we good to go, or is there somethin' else?

MOM. *(Sincere, cheery.)* It's so nice to have everyone together.

JILL. *(Emotional.)* He killed Mr. Peepers.

CARL. He what?

STACY. Who's Mr. Peepers?

MICHAEL. Her pet gerbil.

GRANDMA. Dear Lord.

JILL. He was part of the family.

UNCLE BOB. And a good source of protein.

(He takes a bite of beef jerky.)

JILL. *(Whimpers.)* Ohh.

MICHAEL. I didn't kill him. He ran away.

JILL. You left the door open to his cage.

MICHAEL. I didn't leave the door open, he opened it himself with his little gerbil paws.

STACY. Impossible. They don't have opposable thumbs.

UNCLE BOB. Don't underestimate gerbils.

JILL. How can I ever trust you if you're gonna lie about Mr. Peepers?

MICHAEL. Well, you always said if you love something, let it go.

JILL. *(Emotional.)* I never said that.

GRANDMA. *(To* **MICHAEL.***)* I think Mr. Peepers committed suicide.

(Gestures to **JILL.***)*

JILL. *(Cries.)* Ohh.

MICHAEL. *(To the others, re:* **JILL.***)* It's her hormones.

MOM. Who wants to decorate cookies?

(Bailing, heading into the kitchen.)

UNCLE BOB. I do.

(He follows her into the kitchen.)

MICHAEL. It was just a gerbil.

JILL. How dare you.

*(To **CARL**.)*

I got Mr. Peepers so Michael would learn responsibility like the kind you have when you raise a baby. I guess we know what Michael would do to our baby. Leave the cage door open.

STACY. You would keep your baby in a cage?

JILL. It's a metaphor for our relationship. And right now, our relationship is crawling out of the cage door and getting eaten by a cat.

GRANDMA. *(To **STACY**.)* When did the cat come in?

STACY. So, is your relationship the gerbil or the baby?

GRANDMA. I am not following this.

MICHAEL. We're not gonna be eaten by a cat, honey. We'll figure it out. It'll be just like it was before.

JILL. Remember when you held my hand and kissed me in public?

MICHAEL. *(Thinks.)* No.

JILL. *(Cries.)* Exactly.

MICHAEL. I feel like I'm on trial, here.

CARL. Okay, let's just get to the bottom line. What does Michael have to do to fix things with you?

JILL. *(Holding back tears.)* I don't know.

CARL. Well, at least you have a solid plan.

JILL. Ya think so?

CARL. No! Why does anybody get married?! You can't win!

MICHAEL. You're telling me.

JILL. *(Emotional.)* That's what I'm talking about.

MICHAEL. No, I didn't mean that.

>*(To* **CARL.***)*

It's her hormones.

JILL. If you say that one more time, I will get the garden shears.

GRANDMA. I *knew* I liked her.

MOM. *(Coming out of the kitchen, away from* **UNCLE BOB.***)* Where did you get that other mistletoe?

UNCLE BOB. *(Holding mistletoe over her head, following her.)* I had a backup.

>*(***MOM*** takes the mistletoe from* **UNCLE BOB** *and tosses it behind the bar.)*

MICHAEL. *(To* **JILL.***)* Okay, what can I do to fix things?

JILL. *(To* **CARL.***)* Well, I do have some thoughts on what could fix things, but he needs to figure it out for himself.

CARL. Great idea. Why would you tell him? Communication is overrated. It's much better if you make him guess.

JILL. Do you think?

GRANDMA. *(To the others.)* Does she not know what "sarcasm" is?

JILL. *(Emotional.)* I just wanna make sure he loves me and wants me to come back, and won't be so OCD.

MICHAEL. I'm not OCD.

CARL. *(Jotting in his notepad. To* **MICHAEL.***)* Does "anal-retentive" have a hyphen?

MICHAEL. Well, I prefer the hyphen –

>*(Realizing.)*

Okay, that's not the same as OCD.

GRANDMA. Marriage has no guarantees. If ya want guarantees, marry a car battery.

CARL. *(Ignoring* **GRANDMA.***)* We need to get Stacy's input, here.

(To STACY.*)*

What's your take?

STACY. Do you know what this means? It means that I have reached the top of the sibling food chain in this family.

MOM. *(To* STACY.*)* Ya know, honey, I think some advice might help right now.

GRANDMA. Everybody's lookin' for advice and help these days. We never asked for help. When I was growin' up on the farm, I got thrown from a horse when I was twelve and broke my leg. Set it myself, then walked home.

UNCLE BOB. Why didn't ya ride the horse home?

GRANDMA. The horse had an unfortunate "accident."

UNCLE BOB. Ya killed it?

GRANDMA. No. But he never reproduced again.

UNCLE BOB. *(Impressed.)* Whoa, that is hot. I tell ya, if you were twenty years younger…

GRANDMA. You couldn't handle me *today*.

MICHAEL. Okay, back to us. I'm just looking for clues to work this out, honey.

CARL. It sounds to me like Jill is testing Michael, to see if he's worth staying with.

JILL. Well, if we don't have trust and respect, and don't love each other then why stay together?

CARL. Why do people get married? It's just a bunch of pain and suffering.

STACY. Because love is worth waiting for even if it takes a lifetime. Then, in return, a lifetime of love will be waiting for you.

MOM. Amen.

CARL. You get that on a Hallmark card?

STACY. Shoebox.

UNCLE BOB. I say that love is not letting people spy on you.

(He closes CARL*'s computer.)*

CARL. And you did that because…?

UNCLE BOB. The government is watching our every move. They can see us through your computer. Not to mention the Chinese hackers.

CARL. Chinese hackers?

UNCLE BOB. I told ya not to mention it.

CARL. I think you're a little paranoid, Uncle Bob.

UNCLE BOB. Am I? Right now, the Chinese are loading up all the public storage units in the U.S. with guns and ammo. At a certain time, their government will call every Chinese restaurant, give 'em a code, and they'll get all the guns out of storage and attack us.

JILL. I knew it.

STACY. What's the code?

CARL. Crouching Tiger, Hidden Mushu.

(*CARL holds out his fist.* **STACY** *pounds it.*)

UNCLE BOB. You can laugh, but who's got the underground bunker with a year's supply of beef gerbils?

JILL. (*Whimpers.*) Ohhh.

UNCLE BOB. (*Correcting himself.*) I mean, jerky.

(*Holds a stick of beef jerky out to* **CARL.**)

Want some?

CARL. NO!

UNCLE BOB. (*Putting it away.*) I have a confession to make.

MICHAEL. Oh, I think you've said enough.

CARL. No, let him speak.

(*He takes out the notepad and pen.*)

UNCLE BOB. It's to someone I care for, in case we're keepin' score in our contest.

STACY. This should be good.

UNCLE BOB. Helen, there's something I've wanted to say to you for a long time.

MOM. And I'm sure it's good. Is anybody hungry?

UNCLE BOB. There's a reason I haven't called or been around for a few years.

MOM. Oh, you don't need a reason not to be around.

UNCLE BOB. The reason is, I wanted to give you a little time to mourn before making my intentions known.

CARL. What now? What's happening?

STACY. This is awesome.

UNCLE BOB. I've always had a little thing for Helen… Who knows what would have happened if my brother didn't win her over.

MICHAEL. Are you talking about our dad, who was married to Mom for thirty-five years?

UNCLE BOB. May he rest in peace.

CARL. Is this uncomfortable for anyone else other than me?

MICHAEL. Yes.

MOM. *(Uncomfortable.)* Who wants a drink?

(**GRANDMA** *raises her hand.*)

UNCLE BOB. I don't know if you knew this, but your mom and I dated before she met your dad.

CARL. Whoa.

JILL. Oh, my gosh.

STACY. I didn't know that.

MICHAEL. Crap in a basket.

GRANDMA. That was my prison name.

MOM. Ya know, we really don't have to go into this.

STACY. Yes, we do.

UNCLE BOB. I actually introduced your mom to your dad.

STACY. Wow.

MICHAEL. There's nothing good that's coming outta this story.

UNCLE BOB. He stole her from me.

MOM. Oh, it wasn't exactly like that.

UNCLE BOB. Your mom was so gentle.

MICHAEL. *(He closes his eyes and puts his fingers in his ears so he can't hear.)* La la la la la la la.

UNCLE BOB. Oh, yeah, she used to hold me like a baby chick.

MICHAEL. Is this happening?

UNCLE BOB. She used to wash my hair on Thursdays. Scrub a dub dub.

MICHAEL. Please stop.

MOM. They don't wanna hear about that.

MICHAEL. Nope.

STACY. I do.

UNCLE BOB. Your mom almost didn't marry your dad.

CARL. She what?

MOM. We don't need to go into this.

UNCLE BOB. She had doubts right up to the wedding day.

CARL. Is that true?

UNCLE BOB. Oh, yeah. She was conflicted.

CARL. Conflicted. What does that mean?

GRANDMA. Having feelings that disagree with one another.

CARL. No, I mean…

UNCLE BOB. *(To MOM.)* Would you like to tell 'em?

MOM. No, I would not.

STACY. Tell us.

MOM. *(Holds up the plate of little wieners to the others.)* Wieners?

UNCLE BOB. All I can say is, Michael, you have a lot of my characteristics.

JILL. Whoa.

CARL. Wait, so Michael is your…

MICHAEL. NOOOOOOOOO!

End of Act I

ACT II

(Thirty seconds later.)

MICHAEL. NOOOOOOOOO!

CARL. How many times are you gonna do that?

MICHAEL. Mom, tell me Uncle Bob's not my dad.

MOM. Is it really that important, honey?

MICHAEL. Well, yeah! Because if he's my dad, I can never have children.

(To **UNCLE BOB**.*)*

No offense, but it would be wrong to bring another Uncle Bob into this world.

UNCLE BOB. None taken.

GRANDMA. Why don't you strap on some gourds, there, Nancy. You can have normal kids even if you marry a relative. When I was growin' up, there were no single men in my hometown, so I married my brother.

STACY. Really?

GRANDMA. No! What do you think I am, a freak?

MOM. Well…

GRANDMA. He was my cousin.

MOM, STACY, CARL & MICHAEL. *(Groaning.)* Ohhh.

GRANDMA. Well, not my *first* cousin!

MOM. I think we're gettin' away from our contest, here.

JILL. What are the chances that Michael's child would be, you know…like Uncle Bob?

MICHAEL. I don't wanna take that chance. I'm gonna need a paternity test.

UNCLE BOB. Would ya like a stool sample?

MICHAEL. No, no, just hair would be fine.

(The phone rings.)

MOM. Michael, will you get that?

*(**GRANDMA** goes into the kitchen.)*

MICHAEL. Sure.

(He answers the phone.)

Hello? …It's Michael… Oh, hi, Dr. Hansen, I haven't seen you for awhile. How have you been?

MOM. He's an old friend of the family.

*(**MICHAEL** looks at **MOM**.)*

MICHAEL. Yeah, she's doin' fine. Do you wanna talk to her? …Uh-huh.

*(To **MOM**.)*

He's calling to wish everyone a Merry Christmas.

EVERYONE. Merry Christmas!

MICHAEL. *(Into the phone.)* Yeah, everyone's here… Did she tell me what…

(He gets a somber look.)

Yeah, I work with her primary care physician… Yes, that's correct, I have permission to receive her information…

(He crosses away from everyone.)

She what? …No, I didn't know… Right, right, yeah… Uh-huh…uh-huh…

(He turns away.)

So…what's the prognosis?

*(Everyone looks at **MICHAEL**.)*

Uh-huh…right…yeah…thanks for letting me know. Bye.

(He hangs up.)

*(He looks at **MOM**. Everyone looks at **MOM**. They know something is wrong. **GRANDMA** comes out of the kitchen, notices everyone is somber.)*

GRANDMA. What, did somebody die?

MICHAEL. No, but, Mom, do you have something you'd like to tell everyone?

MOM. *(Thinks.)* Dinner will be ready in about an hour.

MICHAEL. Anything else?

MOM. Oh, the cancer thing. That's no big deal.

CARL. You have cancer?

MICHAEL. She has a tumor in her breast.

JILL. *(Emotional.)* Oh, no.

STACY. Is that true?

MOM. Well, I was gonna tell you next week since this is Christmas, but now that you know...

> (**CARL**, *emotional, hugs* **MOM**. **STACY** *hugs her, too.*)

JILL. *(Emotional.)* I'm so sorry.

UNCLE BOB. Well, that's a turn of events.

MOM. Oh, stop fussing, it's not that bad.

> (**MOM** *goes to the Christmas tree and starts putting decorations on it.*)

CARL. No? Why, is it the good cancer?

MICHAEL. No.

CARL. *(To* **MICHAEL.***)* So, what do we do? What's the next step?

MICHAEL. They did a biopsy and they think they caught it early. He said the chances are good if we treat it right away.

JILL. Well, that's positive. Unless it isn't.

MICHAEL. *(Reassuring her.)* It's positive.

GRANDMA. I already told her she's gonna be fine. I had cancer and I got through it. My hooters tried to kill me, so I got rid of 'em.

> *(Looks at her breasts.)*

Thanks a lot, Thelma and Louise. I got fake ones.

They're not bad. You wanna see?

STACY, CARL, MICHAEL & JILL.	UNCLE BOB.
NO!	YES!

GRANDMA. *(Ignoring* **UNCLE BOB.***)* That was fifteen years ago. You'll be fine. I'll take care of ya.

MOM. That's what I was afraid of.

CARL. How are you feelin', Mom?

MOM. I'm fine. You kids remember to put your ornaments on the tree.

> *(To* **UNCLE BOB.***)*

They all have their own ornament.

> *(She gestures to* **CARL** *and* **STACY** *to put their ornaments on the tree.)*

MICHAEL. She's in denial.

MOM. I'm in what?

MICHAEL. In denial. It's one of the five stages of grief; denial, anger, bargaining, depression, acceptance.

MOM. Can I just skip to the acceptance part?

> *(***CARL** *goes to put his ornament on the tree, from the box under the tree.)*

MICHAEL. Well, they don't always go in the order I described. Sometimes you skip around.

MOM. Then, good. We'll go right to acceptance.

GRANDMA. Acceptance is like a full bladder.

STACY. No idea what that means.

JILL. She's saying that sometimes you just have to let it go.

> *(***STACY** *goes to put her ornament on the tree, from the box under the tree.)*

MICHAEL. *(To the others.)* Mom's in denial.

MOM. No, no, I'm fully on board with what's happening. I just prefer to skip the dramatics.

MICHAEL. It's worse than I thought.

MOM. Oh, look on the bright side. It's taken your mind off of being Uncle Bob's son.

MICHAEL. Until *now*!

MOM. *(Stops hanging ornaments.)* Listen, I'm ready to move on. I've had a great life.

GRANDMA. Better than my life. When I grew up on the farm in Crosby, North Dakota, eight miles from Canada, we had ten kids and two parents in a one-room house. You ever use an outhouse in forty-below weather? I got frostbite on my butt cheeks. Still can't feel 'em.

> *(To* **CARL**, *facing her butt to him.)*

Go ahead, pinch.

CARL.	**UNCLE BOB.**
No, thank you.	Okay.

GRANDMA. *(Ignoring* **UNCLE BOB**.*)* It was a tough life. My mother gave birth to all ten of us by herself.

JILL. Where was your father?

GRANDMA. Out milking the cows.

JILL. He what?!

GRANDMA. Well, they weren't gonna milk themselves.

MICHAEL. I'll take you to the hospital tomorrow, Mom. We'll get you set up with radiation.

JILL. Good idea.

MOM. Oh, you don't have to do that, dear, I'll be fine.

CARL. You should go with Michael, Mom.

MOM. You're not worried, are ya? 'Cause I'm not.

> *(She gestures to* **MICHAEL** *to put his ornament on the tree.)*

MICHAEL. Denial. Come on, Mom, it's amazing the things they can do these days to treat cancer.

> *(He puts his ornament on the tree.)*

STACY. You should do it, Mom.

UNCLE BOB. I hear that smoking the pot makes you feel better... Let me know if ya need any.

>   (*He mimes smoking a joint.*)

MOM. I've had a good life. I really have. Besides, what else am I gonna do? Run with the bulls in Pamplona?

GRANDMA. *I* ran with the bulls in Pamplona.

MOM. I don't remember that.

GRANDMA. Only *they* ran from *me.*

MOM. Now *that* I believe.

UNCLE BOB. What about *me?*

MOM. What *about* you?

UNCLE BOB. You have *me.* That should be *some* incentive.

MOM. (*To* **MICHAEL.**) Is there any way to speed up the cancer?

MICHAEL. Mom, cancer is not something you should joke about.

MOM. What, do you want me to get all sad and despondent? Will that help?

MICHAEL. No.

MOM. Good, then I'll have a sense of humor about it.

UNCLE BOB. I'll cheer you up, Helen.

MOM. (*To* **MICHAEL.**) Why is he still talking?

JILL. Let's sing a Christmas song. That'll lighten things up.
>   ON THE FIRST DAY OF CHRISTMAS.
>   MY TRUE LOVE SENT TO ME.

GRANDMA. (*Sung to the melody of "Five golden rings."*)
>   PLEASE SHOOT ME NOW.

MOM. You don't have to cheer me up.

UNCLE BOB. Come on, Helen. I'm right here. Don't you miss being with a man?

MICHAEL & CARL. (*Groaning.*) Ohh.

UNCLE BOB. You don't get those urges?

GRANDMA. When I got those urges, I went out to the barn and milked the cows.

UNCLE BOB. I'm here for ya, Helen. Anything ya need. Anything at all. I'm a donor if ya need an organ. 'Cause I got an organ I'd like to give ya.

CARL, MICHAEL, STACY & JILL. *(Groaning.)* Ohhh.

UNCLE BOB. My kidney. I got two of 'em.

MOM. Thanks, but I don't need an organ.

UNCLE BOB. Ya might as well take it. Otherwise, I'm just gonna sell it.

MICHAEL. *(Re: UNCLE BOB.)* Is that what I'm gonna turn out like?

CARL. You're already there, buddy.

JILL. You should really get treatment, Helen.

MOM. Oh, honey, death is nature's way of tellin' ya to slow down.

GRANDMA. The Grim Reaper has been knockin' on my door for years, and I have been avoiding him like he's a Jehovah's Witness.

MICHAEL. You're not gonna let Grandma win the longevity race are ya?

MOM. Why not? I'm kinda lookin' forward to seein' your dad again, in Heaven.

CARL. Oh, jeez. Mom, there's plenty of time to see Dad.

UNCLE BOB. How do ya know he went to Heaven? He might of gone up there, rung the buzzer, and no one answered. He might have taken the southbound train, if ya know what I'm sayin'.

(They all look at him.)

"Hell," that's what I'm –

MICHAEL. Yeah, we got it.

UNCLE BOB. I'm just tryin' to be encouraging.

MOM. I got news for you, none of us is gettin' outta this alive.

CARL. I'm kinda surprised, Mom. You're one of the most competitive people I know. It's not like you to give up like this.

MOM. Okay, here's the deal. You would all make me very happy if ya didn't make a big deal outta this, okay. You are *not* gonna feel sorry for me. That's an order. We are gonna have a nice Christmas with our little contest, and we're gonna have prizes. And it's gonna be fun, dammit!

(She smiles.)

JILL. Christmas songs are fun.

GRANDMA. *(Reminiscing.)* When I was your age we sat in front of the fire while Grandpa sang "Jingle Bells" out of the hole in his wind pipe.

JILL.

SO, BRING US SOME FIGGY PUDDING.

GRANDMA. I had figgy pudding once. Cleaned me right out. Now *that* was a "two Depends" day…

(Looks down at her "underwear region" and moves her hips.)

And so is today.

(She exits to the bathroom.)

*(**CARL** types into the computer.)*

STACY. Mom, there's gotta be something you haven't done in life that you wanna do. Don't you have a bucket list?

MOM. I'd like to see Carl make up with Rita and get married.

CARL. Oooh. Wow. Yeah, about that, Mom.

MOM. I think Rita would make a great wife. And she's got those wide birthing hips.

JILL. *(Whimpers.)* Ohh.

CARL. Okay, so…if I get back with Rita, you'll get treatment?

MOM. Yes.

CARL. It's extortion. "Make a wish" extortion.

MOM. Well, you're not workin' that hard on my contest. I figure you need more incentive.

CARL. I thought you didn't wanna make a big deal outta this?

MOM. I make the rules. I can change 'em at any time.

MICHAEL. Carl, you just need to pick up the phone and call Rita. Be direct. Women like that. Be confident, but have a little humility in your voice.

CARL. Ya think?

MICHAEL. I know women.

JILL. Not really.

MICHAEL. Just do it.

MOM. Carl, honey, do you love her?

CARL. Well…

MOM. That's a "yes." Does she make you happy?

CARL. Yeah.

MOM. Then what are you waiting for?

GRANDMA. *(Offstage, from the other room.)* He's waitin' to grow a pair!

UNCLE BOB. Ya might wanna practice first. Try it on me. Go ahead, let's role-play. I'll be Rita. Wait, I gotta get into character.

(With a heavy female southern accent.)

Why, Carl, I do declare.

CARL. She's not southern.

(Takes out his cell, speed dials.)

I'm just gonna call her.

(He heads to the den.)

MICHAEL. Oh, no, you have to do it out here. We have to witness it or it doesn't count.

UNCLE BOB. No pressure.

*(**GRANDMA** enters.)*

CARL. *(Into phone.)* Hey, Rita, it's me. Merry Christmas… Thanks… Okay, so, first of all, I'm sorry I said our relationship was goin' to the Olive Garden, and then to a movie.

(He laughs.)

I mean, it *was* kinda funny. Hello? …She hung up!

STACY. *(Sarcastic.)* Noooo.

CARL. *(Flustered.)* Crap!

(To STACY.)

This is all your fault.

STACY. How's that?

CARL. *(Flustered.)* You and your female species. You make us wanna be with you and have fun, and that's not good enough, is it? You can't just have fun, you wanna get married. I hate you!

(Changes tone, remorseful.)

No, I don't. I'm sorry, I didn't mean that.

(Back to flustered.)

Yes, I did. Because of you and your lady gender, my life is miserable. All I can do is think of Rita. What's Rita doin' now? Is she with another guy? A curse on you! A lady curse!

(Changes tone, remorseful.)

I'm sorry, that was wrong. I take the lady curse back.

(Back to flustered.)

No, I don't! A double lady curse, for ruining my Christmas! I was doin' just fine, then Rita comes into my life, sticks a knife into my heart and twists it with her sneaky lady hands. I hate you!

(Changes tone, remorseful.)

No, I don't, that was harsh, I'm just angry, I'm sorry.

(Back to flustered.)

No, I'm not. You twisted the knife, too. Oh, yeah, your lady hand was on it, too, along with the hands of all lady phylum… I don't know if I'm using that word right, but you know what I mean! All of you twisting that knife, and twisting it…

> *(Emotional, he goes to his knees, ending up lying on the floor in a fetal position.)*

And ripping and twisting and ripping my heart to pieces until I'm a soggy bag of mashed potatoes.

GRANDMA. Will somebody help Carl find his backbone.

UNCLE BOB. *(To* **CARL.**) It's tough to be alone during the holidays. Ya do things you don't normally do. This one Christmas, I took myself hostage and called 911 just to have someone to talk to… That did not end well. Don't ask.

STACY. We won't.

JILL. I was happy a minute ago.

MICHAEL. *(To* **CARL,** *changing the subject.)* Okay, we need to go to Plan B. Grovel. Start cryin', beg to have her come back, she'll respect you for that.

CARL. *(Getting up.)* I think the fat lady has sung.

GRANDMA. I know the fat lady. We used to go out for ice cream, together. And she has not sung. So why don't you take off your Girl Scout outfit, put down the Thin Mints, and put on some man pants, ya gelding.

CARL. I can't force Rita to talk to me.

GRANDMA. What happened to men? We used to have men in this country who would conquer a village, burn it down, and take no prisoners.

MOM. Those were the Vikings.

GRANDMA. *(To* **CARL.**) You need to conquer her lady village.

CARL. Mom, is there anything else on your Christmas "make a wish" list we can do to get you to go to treatment?

MOM. Well, I'd like Michael and Jill to get back together and have a baby.

JILL. *(Emotional.)* Ohh.

MICHAEL. Oh, wow, umm…is there anything on your list that Stacy can do?

GRANDMA. Is Stacy here?

(**STACY** *raises her hand.*)

MOM. Stacy. Well, let me think…she has a baby, so we're good with that. She's gay, so we're covered there.

GRANDMA. Is that reversible?

STACY. No.

MOM. She has a good job. What do you do again?

STACY. I'm an environmental hydroponic engineer.

GRANDMA. Gesundheit.

(*She laughs, no one else laughs.*)

'Cause it sounded like a sneeze…

(*No one is laughing.*)

Tough room.

UNCLE BOB. What's an environmental whatcha callit?

STACY. (*Surprised he would ask.*) Oh, yeah, well, right now I'm calibrating the controllers that automate the measurements for the hydroponic system, using electrical conductivity to balance the levels of alkalines, O2 and pH tolerance.

UNCLE BOB. Didn't understand a word of that.

MOM. Yeah, I would say that Stacy is the least of my worries.

UNCLE BOB. What about me? Is there anything on your "make a wish" list for me?

MOM. You need to make up with your son.

GRANDMA. What's the deal with your son?

UNCLE BOB. Oh, somethin' about me not bein' around when he was growing up.

GRANDMA. Well, boo-hoo. My parents weren't around and I turned out just fine.

MOM. Well…

GRANDMA. You know what my parents gave me for Christmas one year? Smallpox.

JILL. (*Thinks.*) How did they wrap it?

MICHAEL. Okay, ya know what, I'll do something unselfish right now.

CARL. Is it unselfish if you're doing it to win a contest?

MICHAEL. It's probably on Mom's "make a wish" list, too.

MOM. Go ahead, Michael.

MICHAEL. Okay, here we go. One of the things I have to do for the program –

CARL. What program?

MICHAEL. AA. Part of my healing, is –

GRANDMA. *(Groans.)* Ohh.

MICHAEL. Is to share my feelings and make amends with the ones I hurt.

GRANDMA. Don't do it, Twinkle Toes. Bottle it up. Deny your feelings, lock 'em down and man up for once.

MOM. Grandma, let him share.

STACY. Feelings are a normal human emotion, Grandma.

GRANDMA. Feelings are like water skiing with a fishing pole.

STACY. What does that even mean?

JILL. She's saying you don't need feelings, unless you get hungry while you're water skiing.

(**STACY** *rolls her eyes.*)

MOM. Go ahead, Michael. Make amends.

GRANDMA. Where did my family go? Where are they? Oh, there they are, they took the Wimpy Train to Pansy Town.

MICHAEL. This is really hard for me.

UNCLE BOB. *(Holding up the whiskey.)* Want a shot of liquid courage?

MICHAEL. No, see, the point of the program is *not* to drink.

UNCLE BOB. Your loss.

(*He takes a swig.*)

MOM. Bob, maybe you'd like something less strong. How about some red wine?

UNCLE BOB. I don't drink red wine since the government started planting microchips in the sulfites for their mind control experiments.

JILL. *(Re: her own experience with red wine.)* No wonder.

GRANDMA. Has Bob been smokin' the reefer?

MICHAEL. Grandma, we're all in a safe place right now.

GRANDMA. A "safe place"?

> *(To* **MOM.***)*

Was he adopted?

MICHAEL. Okay, Grandma, that's not very –

> *(To* **MOM.***)*

Was I?

MOM. No.

MICHAEL. *(Moving on.)* Alright, so, Stacy, I know I probably wasn't the best brother to you.

MOM. Michael, you don't have to –

STACY. Sure, he does. Go ahead.

MICHAEL. I know I may have, you know, ignored you when we were kids, and I never wanted to throw the football with you, or watch women's basketball, or go to that k.d. lang concert, or –

> *(Realizing.)*

Oh, yeah, how did I not see that? ...Anyway, I'm sorry about that. I still don't wanna do anything with you, but I'm sorry... So, we're good now?

STACY. Wow, I'm getting a little emotional.

MICHAEL. You are?

STACY. Not at all.

MICHAEL. Okay, okay, I get it. You wanna spend more time with me.

STACY. Ya know, I'm just fine with the amount of time we spend together.

MICHAEL. We don't spend *any* time together.

STACY. Isn't it great?

MICHAEL. So, we're good then?

STACY. Yup. We are amended.

CARL. Okay, me, now.

MICHAEL. Okay, Carl. I'm sorry I took your bike, sold it for cash, and told you it was stolen.

CARL. That was you?!

MICHAEL. No, see, it's okay now, cause I'm apologizing.

CARL. No, it isn't.

MICHAEL. Okay, here's the deal. I got twenty bucks when I sold your bike, so I'm gonna buy you another bike for twenty dollars. Even-steven.

CARL. You can't get a bike for twenty…how about just giving me the twenty bucks?

MICHAEL. No, it has to be what I took.

MOM. Honey, the only one you have to make amends to is your wife.

CARL. Hold on, there. We're not done with me yet.

MOM. I'll get you a new bike, Carl.

CARL. No, that's okay, Mom. I'll take his twenty-dollar bike.

MOM. *(To MICHAEL.)* Very good, Michael. You're in the lead. Keep going.

CARL. *(Groans.)* Ohh.

MICHAEL. Okay, so, Jill, honey, I know sometimes I haven't been as understanding as I could be when you start crying –

JILL. *(Cries.)* Ohh.

MICHAEL. Oh, for crap sake.

> *(JILL shoots him a look.)*

No, see, that was involuntary. Let me start over. Jill, honey, you mean the world to me, and –

JILL. *(Cries.)* Ohh.

MICHAEL. Oh, for the love of…

> *(JILL shoots him a look. He changes his tone.)*

And when you left me –

GRANDMA. She left you?

MICHAEL. Yeah, for three months. We talked about that.

GRANDMA. If I have to pay attention to everything that goes on here…

MICHAEL. When you left me, even though I could play golf whenever I wanted to and sit on the couch in my underwear and have a beer and a pizza and hang out with the guys, and play Nintendo and watch every *Transformer* movie without judgment… I forgot where I was goin' with this.

UNCLE BOB. *(To MICHAEL.)* That sounds great. We should hang out sometime. I'll call ya.

MICHAEL. *(Ignoring BOB, to JILL.)* What I'm trying to say is, you complete me.

STACY. He just went "Jerry McGuire."

MOM. In your own words, Michael.

MICHAEL. I promise to be more open with my feelings, and to say the "L" word at least once a year…

> *(**MOM** clears her throat.)*

Once a month.

> *(**MOM** clears her throat.)*

Once a day.

> *(To himself.)*

Dammit.

JILL. You could tell me you love me, *now*.

GRANDMA. Whoa, whoa, whoa, this isn't Woodstock.

MICHAEL. I just don't wanna be like Dad.

CARL. The man who loved his wife so much, he almost told her.

> *(**JILL** laughs, then cries.)*

MICHAEL. *(Consoling JILL.)* It's okay, honey, it's just your horm–

(JILL *shoots* MICHAEL *a look.*)

Not sayin' a word.

GRANDMA. *(To* MICHAEL.*)* Your problem is you were hugged too much as a child. You're soft. Some advice, if you ever have children, don't hug 'em. It just makes 'em weak. Like your mom did to you.

MOM. *(Changing the subject.)* I have cancer.

GRANDMA. It's not always about you, dear… Now, let's get to what's important.

(*To* MICHAEL.)

Where are you on the whole baby thing? Are ya havin' problems down there?

MICHAEL. No, no, the thing is, we've had a lot of stress and we just need a few weeks away to relax. I think that would help.

GRANDMA. What about that in vitro test tube baby deal? I hear you can order off the menu, blue eyes, blonde hair, Lutheran.

MICHAEL. In vitro is not guaranteed, and it's expensive.

GRANDMA. Well, don't spend any more money on *Dukes of Hazzard* plates.

JILL. Or online gambling.

CARL. Gambling?!

MICHAEL. I'm done with all that.

UNCLE BOB. What about adopting? I got a couple kids you can have.

MICHAEL. We tried. It's not easy to adopt.

GRANDMA. Then get busy! I'd like six great-grandchildren by the time I'm a hundred.

(*Looking up.*)

That's right, Grim Reaper! I will be twerking 'til I'm a hundred.

(She twerks. **UNCLE BOB** *takes a picture of her twerking with his cell phone.)*

Here ya go, walk the dog, paddle the canoe, bake the cookies, and…

(One final thrust.)

Bam!

MOM, STACY, CARL, MICHAEL & JILL. *(Groaning.)* Ohhh.

UNCLE BOB. *(Looking at the photo on his cell phone.)* That's my new screen saver.

MOM. I plan on dying much younger.

STACY. You're not gonna die, Mom.

MOM. Don't take that away from me. It's all I have to look forward to.

GRANDMA. Are we gonna eat some time? I'm starting to hallucinate.

MOM. It's your circulation. Loosen your bra.

GRANDMA. What bra?

CARL, MICHAEL, STACY & JILL. *(Groaning.)* Ohhh!

*(***UNCLE BOB*** takes another photo of* **GRANDMA.***)*

MICHAEL. Before we eat, I have a present for Jill I'd like to give her, if that's okay.

GRANDMA. I thought we were gonna do that *after* dinner?

MOM. Let's try something new, Grandma. A new tradition.

GRANDMA. I like the old traditions.

JILL. I have a family tradition. Let's all hold hands and say what Christmas means to you.

GRANDMA. Count me out, Gidget.

JILL. *(Politely correcting her.)* It's Jill.

GRANDMA. Pretty sure it's "Gidget."

MICHAEL. *(He hands* **JILL** *an envelope.)* Go ahead, open it.

JILL. *(Opens it.)* Oh, it's a trip. An all expense paid two-week vacation to the Ritz-Carlton in Bali.

STACY. Oh, how nice.

GRANDMA. The song, "Bali High" was about me.

MOM. No, it wasn't.

MICHAEL. Just what you wanted, right, to relax and work on having a baby.

JILL. Well…

MICHAEL. I think if we just get away from all the pressure, it'll happen. I mean, I won't be disappointed if it *doesn't* happen, but we can't give up, right? That is, if you'll have me back.

JILL. How did you pay for this?

MICHAEL. I sold my plate collection.

JILL. You sold *all* of 'em?

MICHAEL. *(Sad.)* Yes.

JILL. Captain Kirk petting the Tribbles?

MICHAEL. *(More sad.)* Yes!

JILL. Chewbacca on roller skates?

MICHAEL. *(Even more sad.)* Yes!!

JILL. The Beatles fighting the Rolling Stones with laser swords?

MICHAEL. *(Crying.)* YES!

JILL. That was your favorite one.

MICHAEL. *(Crying.)* I know.

JILL. I *do* mean something to you.

MICHAEL. You mean the world to me.

JILL. *(Whimpers.)* Ohh.

STACY. Did he actually say something nice?

> (**JILL** *holds her hand up, palm toward* **MICHAEL**, *and does the "Vulcan Salute," a.k.a. "Spock hand gesture," with her fingers parted between the middle and ring finger.* **MICHAEL** *does the same. They touch hands.*)

JILL & MICHAEL. *(Upon touching hands, they gasp in pleasure.)* Ahhh.

GRANDMA. This just got really weird.

MOM. Oh, they're back together.

JILL. I got somethin' for you, too.

>   *(She hands him the present she brought in.)*

MICHAEL. *(Opening the box.)* What is it?

GRANDMA. Why do they always ask what it is before opening it?

MICHAEL. *(Sees what's inside.)* It's the limited edition *Star Trek* Captain series commemorative plate, and it's signed!

JILL. It was the last in the series you needed to complete your collection.

UNCLE BOB. You mean, the collection that he just sold?

MICHAEL. It must have been expensive.

JILL. I used the money that we were saving for in vitro.

CARL. This story sounds familiar.

MICHAEL. You used the baby money for me? For the plate?

JILL. Yeah. I know how important it is to you.

MOM. Well, you don't need in vitro if you make a baby in Bali.

JILL. The thing is, it's too late for that.

MICHAEL. Too late? Are you divorcing me?

JILL. I'm pregnant.

MICHAEL. Who's the father? I'll kill him! Is it Carl?!

JILL. You're the father. You're gonna be a dad.

MICHAEL. Are you serious?

JILL. Yes.

STACY. It's a miracle baby!

JILL. No, it's Michael's.

STACY. Oh.

UNCLE BOB. So, you don't need the trip to Bali.

CARL. This is like, *The Gift of the Magi*, only with "Chewbacca" plates.

>   *(He writes something in his notepad.)*

UNCLE BOB. What are ya writin', there, Carl?

CARL. Oh, nothin'.

MOM. *(To* **JILL**.*)* Oh, my gosh, I'm so happy for you!

　　　(She hugs **JILL**.*)*

UNCLE BOB. Yeah, congratulations!

　　　(**STACY** *hugs* **JILL**.*)*

STACY. That's why you've been crying, isn't it?

JILL. Yeah. All the hormones from being pregnant are makin' me crazy, giving me the "baby brains."

CARL. That's why she understands Grandma.

GRANDMA. Watch it, Peter Pan.

STACY. *(To* **JILL**.*)* You're gonna be a great mother.

JILL. Thanks.

STACY. Let me know if there's anything I can do to help. I can babysit, or run errands, or whatever ya need.

JILL. Oh, my gosh, thanks, I really appreciate that.

STACY. We need to plan the baby shower. Have you barfed yet?

JILL. Every day.

STACY. Oh, it gets worse.

JILL. Great.

STACY. We'll talk.

MICHAEL. Okay, wait, so…you knew awhile ago that you were pregnant?

JILL. Yeah.

STACY. *(Trying to calm the pending storm.)* So happy for you.

MICHAEL. And you didn't mention it until now?

JILL. Uh-huh.

MOM. Happy, happy, happy!

JILL. I wanted to make sure we were back together before telling you.

MICHAEL. You wanted to what?!

MOM. Back together. Yaaay!

MICHAEL. What if we weren't back together? You wouldn't tell me?

JILL. Well…

MICHAEL. You wouldn't. You only came back for my money.

JILL. What?!

MOM. Who wants wieners?!

MICHAEL. *(Emotional.)* I just feel so…used.

> *(He cries.)*

GRANDMA. Can I get you a tampon?

MICHAEL. *(Cries.)* Ohhh!

> *(He runs into the den.)*

CARL. *(To* JILL.*)* "You came back for his money"? Where'd he get *that* idea?

JILL. *(Cries.)* Ohhh!

> *(She runs into the kitchen.)*

STACY. I saw that playing out a whole different way.

MOM. They'll work things out.

GRANDMA. Doubtful.

CARL. You know, I'm gonna be positive and say we can still salvage this Christmas. What do you say, Mom?

MOM. Sure. You can still get back with Rita.

CARL. She doesn't wanna see me.

MOM. You know what you have to do. You have to tell her the forbidden words. Go ahead.

CARL. Oh, Mom.

MOM. It's okay, Carl. I'm dying, but take your time.

> *(CARL doesn't move.)*

Take alllll the time in the world.

> *(CARL takes out his phone and hits speed dial.)*

CARL. Okay, alright, I'm calling her.

> *(Into the phone.)*

Hey, Rita, it's me again. How's it goin'? ...Oh, just callin' to say hi... Hey, did you see the Vikings game? Hello? ...She hung up.

STACY. Well, duh.

CARL. *(To STACY.)* It's all your fault.

STACY. Is there anything else on your list, Mom?

MOM. Bob, call your son.

UNCLE BOB. Easier said than done.

> *(Taking out his cell phone.)*

MOM. Go ahead. It's not too late.

UNCLE BOB. I'm afraid I'll get the same response as Carl.

> *(He hits speed dial.)*

MOM. No risk, no reward.

GRANDMA. Is what I told Sir Edmund Hillary the night he scaled my twin peaks.

MOM. Good Lord.

UNCLE BOB. *(Into the phone.)* Hey, Gary, it's your dad, Merry Christmas... Okay, just hear me out for one minute, please... Look, I ahh, I know I wasn't the best dad, I made a lot of mistakes and I let you down, and I'm sorry for that. I just... It would just be great to see ya again, and to see my grandchildren...uh-huh...uh-huh.

> *(After a beat, he takes the phone from his ear, disappointed.)*

He doesn't wanna see me.

MOM. Oh, I'm sorry.

UNCLE BOB. Oh, it's my fault. I should have gotten custody when he was a kid, and I didn't. I abandoned him.

GRANDMA. Apologizing is like riding a porcupine.

STACY. No idea.

JILL. *(Sticks her head out of the kitchen.)* She's saying, it hurts unless the porcupine is all drugged up and has no porkers.

(Goes back in the kitchen.)

STACY. Of course.

UNCLE BOB. *(To* **STACY.***)* My son's middle name is Carl, named after your dad. I was so proud of my brother. I always looked up to him. He had it all, great life, great family. He got the prettiest girl in town.

(He looks at **MOM.***)*

MOM. *(Blushing.)* Oh, stop.

UNCLE BOB. Okay.

MOM. No, go on.

UNCLE BOB. He got Helen, and I ended up with three hags who took me for everything.

GRANDMA. You ain't no prize, either, Uncle Whiskey Breath.

UNCLE BOB. Everyone envied Carl. He was my best friend. I remember I got in big trouble once. He bailed me out, put me into rehab. I hoped my son would grow up to be just like him.

STACY. Did he?

UNCLE BOB. Oh, no. That's okay. Big shoes to fill… Oh, hey, your dad sent me an email about a month before he died. You want me to read it?

CARL. Sure.

*(***BOB*** starts to read it to himself, moving his lips.)*

Can you read it out loud?

UNCLE BOB. Oh, yeah, sure.

(Looks at his phone, reads.)

Hey Bob, I'm really proud of you for goin' through rehab. You might wanna think about finding someone and settling down again. I know it's not easy to find someone as terrific as my Helen, but when you do find the right girl, it's worth all the tough times. I don't know how I ever deserved someone as wonderful as Helen.

(To **MOM.***)*

He always had to rub it in.

(Reading the email.)

I want you to know that I'll always be there for ya, buddy. Anything ya need, just let me know. Your brother, Carl…

(He sets the phone on the dining table. Emotional.)

When he died, I just lost it… He was my anchor, my rock…and he was gone. So, I started drinking again, and then my son stopped talkin' to me.

MOM. Do you want your son back?

UNCLE BOB. Yeah.

GRANDMA. *(Stern.)* Then sober up! Give him somethin' to be proud of. Right now you're an embarrassment to him.

UNCLE BOB. *(Sadly.)* Yeah, I know… Ya know, I think I'll, ahh… I'll go check my email.

(He exits to the den in shame, without his cell phone.)

MOM. *(To* **GRANDMA.***)* How can you be so mean?

GRANDMA. It's not that hard. I was raised Lutheran.

CARL. Is it me or did Uncle Bob just…become a different person?

STACY. Alcoholics can sometimes put up a false exterior to cover up what's going on inside.

*(***GRANDMA*** grabs* **UNCLE BOB***'s cell phone and heads toward the kitchen.)*

MOM. Where are you goin'?

GRANDMA. Bob forgot his cell phone. He'll need it.

MOM. He went in the den…

*(***GRANDMA*** disappears into the kitchen.)*

Now, Grandma, don't mess it up!

STACY. Mom, was Dad proud of me?

MOM. Oh, my gosh, honey, yes, he was so proud of you. You were such a wonderful daughter, and a great student and the work that you do and being able to take care of yourself. I know he was sorry he didn't spend more time with you growing up, but he loved you so much.

STACY. Thanks.

CARL. Was Dad proud of *me?*

MOM. Not at all.

    (CARL reacts.)

I'm joking. Of course he was proud of you. You know that. And then you became a journalist and, well... that's what killed him.

CARL. Mom!

MOM. What happened to your sense of humor? Seriously. He loved you very much even though he never said it while he was alive.

CARL. It was implied.

MOM. He showed his love through his actions. He was a great provider, he gave us everything we needed.

STACY. I miss Dad, even though he never hugged me or said he loved me.

MOM. I miss that, too, honey... Well, I guess I won't be goin' to treatment. That's okay, it makes you so sick.

CARL. Well, it's better than the alternative.

STACY. You should go, Mom. You wanna see your grandchildren grow up, don't you?

MOM. *(Smiles.)* How's your friend?

STACY. Fine.

    (GRANDMA comes out of the kitchen and puts UNCLE BOB's cell phone back on the table.)

MOM. Why don't you call her and wish her a Merry Christmas.

STACY. *(Looks at GRANDMA.)* Oh, yeah, not sure that's a good idea with...

    (She spells it out.)

G-r-a-n-d-m-a in the room.

GRANDMA. I can spell, ya door knob.

MOM. That's okay, honey, you don't have to call her, even though I'd like ya to... Did I tell you I'm dying?

STACY. Okay, okay, I'll call her.

(She takes out her phone and hits speed dial.)

GRANDMA. Sure are a lot of phone calls today.

MOM. Well, it's Christmas. It's what you do.

STACY. *(Into phone.)* Hey, Merry Christmas... Yeah, it's been...interesting. How about you? ...Uh-huh. How are your folks? ...Did you, ahh, did you tell 'em? ...You said you would... Well, just go ahead and do it... No, I don't wanna argue...

(She takes the phone away from her ear.)

CARL. Did she hang up?

*(**STACY** doesn't answer.)*

She hung up. You're not infallible. You have problems, too. I just moved up the sibling food chain.

(He goes to his laptop and types.)

STACY. So happy I could brighten your day.

GRANDMA. This whole evening feels like we're on the Titanic. I did *not* enjoy that cruise.

STACY. What are you working on, there, Carl?

CARL. Oh, I have to write an article about Christmas.

STACY. What about Christmas?

CARL. Oh, you know, family Christmas stuff.

STACY. Can I see?

(She takes his computer.)

CARL. Hey, gimme that back.

*(**STACY** runs down the hall, goes into the bathroom, and locks the door. **CARL** follows.)*

Would you come outta there! Mom, Stacy took my computer and locked herself in the bathroom.

(**MICHAEL** *comes out of the den.*)

GRANDMA. Would you like me to tell your little sister to stop being mean?

CARL. Yeah, would you?

GRANDMA. Okay, while I do that, why don't you go play with your Barbie dolls, ya pantywaist.

(**STACY** *comes out of the bathroom with* **CARL**'s *computer.*)

STACY. Carl, is there something you'd like to tell everyone about your article?

(*Hands the computer to* **CARL**.)

CARL. No.

MICHAEL. What article?

STACY. It seems that Carl is writing an article for his newspaper about our family.

MICHAEL. What about our family?

(**JILL** *enters from the kitchen.*)

CARL. Oh, you know, Christmas with our family. It's no big deal.

STACY. With personal details about us.

MICHAEL. What kind of details?

(*He grabs the computer from* **CARL** *and reads.*)

CARL. No, don't read that. That's private.

MICHAEL. (*Reading.*) So, you're writing about me and Jill being separated and the rehab thing and making amends, and Mom's cancer, Uncle Bob who may be my dad, Grandma being certifiable.

CARL. Not my words, Grandma.

MICHAEL. And everything we need to know about Stacy.

(*To* **CARL**.)

Everyone in Minneapolis will read this.

(He hands the computer back to **CARL***.)*

CARL. Well, not everyone. I mean, I wish.

STACY. Don't you think what you're writing is a little personal?

CARL. Would you like me to change the names?

STACY. People will still know who you're referring to.

CARL. No, they won't.

STACY. I'll know.

CARL. Well...what exactly is your concern?

STACY. My concern? I guess I just don't want the world to know about my lifestyle.

CARL. No one cares anymore. It's not a big deal. Everyone is okay with it.

STACY. Not everyone.

CARL. Well, that's their problem.

STACY. And LaKeesha wouldn't want anyone to read about her, either.

CARL. For the same reason?

STACY. She hasn't come out to her parents yet.

CARL. Well, she just needs to tell 'em.

STACY. I thought she was going to, today.

MOM. I bet they're more open-minded than you think.

STACY. The point is, I don't want Carl to write about me. I'm guessing everybody else here feels the same way.

CARL. Is that true? Does everybody else feel the same way?

(No one says anything.)

Well, that throws a wrench into things.

*(***CARL*** takes out his phone.)*

STACY. I'm surprised that you thought it was okay to do that.

CARL. Okay, okay, I'm sorry, I'll fix it. I'll just...text my editor and tell him I don't have a story.

(He types in the text on his phone.)

GRANDMA. Well, it's official. This Christmas is circling the bowl. Flush! Right down the Mississippi.

(Calling out.)

Mark Twain!

(To **CARL.***)*

I used to crew for him.

MOM. *(To* **GRANDMA.***)* Are you sure we're related?

*(***UNCLE BOB** *enters. He retrieves his phone from the table.)*

CARL. *(He hits "send" on the text.)* I guess I'll just go back to driving a truck for Pillsbury.

MOM. I'm sorry, honey.

CARL. Doesn't matter. What matters is, we get you treated.

MOM. We still have a couple unfinished things. Michael, is there something you wanted to say to Jill? I mean, she *is* the mother of your child.

*(***MICHAEL** *doesn't say anything.)*

Or, you could help me write my obituary.

GRANDMA. "She's survived by her ungrateful son, Michael."

MICHAEL. Okay, okay.

(To **JILL.***)*

In the den, honey?

(He starts toward the den.)

JILL. Yeah, sure.

CARL. Oh, no, out here or it doesn't count.

MICHAEL. *(Stopping.)* I'm sorry, Jill. I was just kind of emotional, hearing about the baby, and… I just thought you came back for my money.

JILL. I don't care about your money. I just wanna be with you.

CARL. *WHY?!*

>   (*Everyone glares at* **CARL.**)

   Did I say that out loud?

UNCLE BOB. Well, I believe her. She could leave right now and take half. I know.

MICHAEL. Can you forgive me?

JILL. Of course.

MICHAEL. I love you.

JILL. I love you, too.

>   (*They kiss and hug.*)

STACY. (*How sweet.*) Ohh.

GRANDMA. Finally.

MICHAEL. I just hope we don't have an Uncle Bob baby.

UNCLE BOB. Sweet!

MOM. Uncle Bob is *not* your father.

MICHAEL. How do you know?

MOM. Well, aside from the fact that we never had…

>   (*Spells it out, whispering it.*)

   S. E. X.

JILL. (*Cheerful.*) Yaay.

MICHAEL. And that's not something you thought you should mention about an hour ago when I was freaking out?

MOM. I wanted to see how you would handle it.

MICHAEL. Thanks. Did I pass?

MOM. Well…

MICHAEL. And Uncle Bob, you actually thought I was your son?

UNCLE BOB. No, I never thought that. I just said you have a lot of my characteristics.

MICHAEL. Well, why didn't you just say that? Ahh!

STACY. Best Christmas ever.

MOM. And I never had second thoughts about your dad when we got married. He got a little nervous, but I guess that runs in the family. Right, Carl?

(*She looks at* **CARL**.)

CARL. Is everyone testing everybody else today?

MOM. Well, isn't Christmas like a test? "Have you been a good little boy? If not, no presents for you!"

STACY. Are you having fun, Mom?

MOM. Oh, yeah.

MICHAEL. Can we schedule the radiation, now?

MOM. Not quite yet.

(*She looks at* **CARL**.)

Carl?

CARL. Oh, for sittin' on the cat. She doesn't wanna talk to me.

MOM. She does if you say the right thing.

JILL. She's right, Carl.

GRANDMA. You want someone to hold your hand, cupcake?

CARL. (*He takes out his phone and pushes speed dial.*) Yeah, actually, I do.

GRANDMA. Ain't gonna happen, Tinker Bell.

CARL. (*Into the phone.*) Rita, hi. Don't hang up, please. I have somethin' really important to say to you… Thanks… Okay, here goes…umm…

(*He tries to say "I love you" to Rita, but he can't.*)

I lluuhhh… I lluuhhh. Hello? …She hung up!

STACY. Shocker.

GRANDMA. Call her back!

(**CARL** *redials.*)

MOM. Tell her the forbidden words!

GRANDMA. *DO IT!*

CARL. (*Into the phone.*) I LOVE YOU!

(*Everyone gasps. After a beat.*)

Are ya still there? …You are? …Wow, okay, umm… "Say it again"?

(He looks around. Everyone is looking at him. He whispers.)

I love you… Yeah, everyone is listening… Oh, come on…okay, okay…

(Loud.)

I love you… "Slower and with more meaning"?

(Puts his hand over the phone. To STACY, whispering.)

I hate you.

(Into the phone.)

No, no, no, not you. Look, I'm only happy when I'm with you, okay. Why don't I tell you how I feel about you, slowly and with more meaning over dinner. How does that sound? …No, not the Olive Garden… Really? You will? …Thank you. I'll call you tomorrow. Say hi to your folks… They hate me? Okay, never mind. Talk to you tomorrow. Merry Christmas. Bye.

(Hangs up. Everyone applauds.)

JILL. Good for you, Carl.

CARL. Okay, Mom, time to schedule your treatment.

MOM. Well…

CARL. *(He goes to MOM, emotional.)* C'mon, Mom, do it for us, and for your grandchildren. You're all we have now.

GRANDMA. You have *me*.

CARL. *(Looks at GRANDMA for a beat, then back to MOM.)* You're all we have now… We can't lose you. We need you around a little longer. Your work isn't done yet… Look, Mom, you raised three good kids, okay.

(Looks at MICHAEL.)

Well, two out of three. And we need you to be our guiding light when we go off track, you know, to be there and encourage us when we get down.

MOM. Carl, honey, I'm not gonna be here to watch over you forever. What's important is that you take care of yourself, be responsible, and do good things for other people when I'm gone.

CARL. *(Emotional.)* Mom, you're my rock. You're the only reason I'm even keeping it together right now... You are the only person on this planet who loves me unconditionally. Please don't take that away from me...

> (**MOM** *doesn't respond.*)

C'mon, Mom, you have so many more good years ahead of you –

MOM. I made an appointment.

CARL. You what?

MOM. For treatment. I made an appointment, yesterday.

JILL. *(Cheerful.)* Yaay.

CARL. And you still wanted us to go through with your "make a wish" scavenger hunt?

MOM. Well, did it hurt anyone?

CARL. No.

STACY. We're glad you made the appointment, Mom.

JILL. *(Cheerful.)* Yaay.

MOM. Do you really think I'm gonna let cancer beat me? Seriously, I won twenty-one club championships. I survived my mother.

GRANDMA. You're welcome.

MOM. *(To* **CARL.***)* And thank you for the nice words, honey.

> *(To everyone.)*

Okay, I have the results of the contest.

CARL. I thought we had 'til midnight.

MOM. I make the rules, I can change 'em at any time.

UNCLE BOB. *(Looking at his cell phone.)* Hey, what do ya know. I just got a text from my son.

GRANDMA. What did he say?

UNCLE BOB. *(Looking at the phone.)* He wants to talk. He's gonna call me tomorrow.

JILL. Well, that's positive. Unless it isn't.

UNCLE BOB. No, it's good. He sent a smiley face emoji.

*(**UNCLE BOB** texts him back.)*

MOM. *(To **GRANDMA**.)* Did you?

(Call his son.)

GRANDMA. Did I what?

MOM. Nothing.

*(Smiles at **GRANDMA**, who taps the side of her nose with her index finger like they did in* The Sting. **MOM** *reciprocates the gesture.* **CARL** *sees it. To* **UNCLE BOB**.*)*

I'm really happy for you.

UNCLE BOB. Can I have a kiss?

MOM. No.

UNCLE BOB. Crap... I guess a sleepover is outta the question.

MICHAEL, CARL, STACY & JILL. *(Groaning.)* Ohhh.

CARL. Ya know what, I think we did everything on Mom's "make a wish" list.

STACY. *(Looking at her cell phone.)* Well, this is interesting. LaKeesha just came out to her parents.

CARL. Were they okay with it?

STACY. Yeah. She said they knew.

CARL. Well, that's good.

STACY. Apparently, someone told 'em.

*(She looks at **MOM**.)*

MOM. I wonder who?

STACY. Thanks, Mom.

*(**GRANDMA** smiles at **MOM**, who taps the side of her nose with her index finger like they did in* The

Sting. **GRANDMA** *reciprocates the gesture.* **CARL** *sees it.*)

CARL. Look at Mom and Grandma, the two conspirators. They're like Butch Cassidy and the Sundance Kid.

GRANDMA. I used to ride bikes with Butch Cassidy.

MOM. No, ya didn't. Why do I even bother?

GRANDMA. Well, now that my gay granddaughter is back with her partner, my Christmas is complete.

STACY. *(Goes to hug her, endearing.)* Ohh.

GRANDMA. *(Giving in to the hug.)* Okay, okay.

(*She gives* **STACY** *an arm around the shoulder, side hug.*)

STACY. Oh, a side hug.

JILL. *(How sweet.)* Ohh.

MOM. That's more than I ever got.

GRANDMA. Oh, I hugged you when you were born, you just don't remember.

MOM. Mother of the Year.

CARL. Looks like everything kinda fell into place for everyone.

JILL. Just like, *It's a Wonderful Life.*

GRANDMA. Not if you have shingles.

MOM. Okay then, back to the contest. This has been my favorite Christmas ever. Well, except for the years that I *didn't* have cancer. And since you've all been so good…

(*Looks at* **GRANDMA.**)

Relatively, I'd like to announce that I am giving all of you…a family cruise for seven days!

(*Everyone looks at* **MOM** *in silence, stunned, for a few beats. Then.*)

STACY. Together?

MOM. Yeah, together.

CARL. All of us, together, for seven days?

MOM. Isn't it great?

MICHAEL. On the same boat?

MOM. *(Stern.)* Yeah, on the same boat!

CARL, MICHAEL & STACY. *(Unenthusiastic, insincere.)* Awesome, great, really excited, can't wait. *(Etc.)*

GRANDMA Can I get a gift certificate instead?

MOM. No. We're all going. Even Bob.

UNCLE BOB. Oh, I'll have to get a new Speedo.

EVERYONE. *(Groaning.)* Ohhh!

MICHAEL. Mom, who's the grand prize winner?

GRANDMA. Before ya answer that, I have a present for the kids. Michael...

> *(She hands a card to **MICHAEL**.)*

You're one of my top three grandchildren.

MICHAEL. You only have three grandchildren.

GRANDMA. And Carl...

> *(Hands a card to **CARL**.)*

Someday you'll be a man.

> *(**CARL** reacts.)*

And Stacy...

> *(Hands a card to **STACY**.)*

It may not have come from your dad's side.

> *(She winks at **STACY**.)*
>
> *(They open their cards.)*

STACY. Grandma, you don't have to give us anything.

MOM. *(To **UNCLE BOB**.)* Every year Grandma gives 'em a five dollar bill.

STACY. Why don't you use the money for yourself, Grandma.

MICHAEL. *(Looking inside the card.)* There's no money.

CARL. *(Looking inside the card.)* Grandma, I'm a little confused. What does "O-W 5" mean?

MICHAEL. Mine says "O-W 4."

STACY. *(Looking at her card.)* "O-W 6."

GRANDMA. Well, ya know I kept the farm up there in Crosby, North Dakota.

CARL. Yeah.

GRANDMA. Well, a few years ago they discovered oil on the farm.

MICHAEL. Oil?

GRANDMA. Yeah, the farm is in the Bakken oil range up there.

UNCLE BOB. How much oil?

GRANDMA. I got ten wells so far.

UNCLE BOB. Ten?! So far?!

STACY. *(To* **MOM**.*)* Did you know about this?

MOM. Oh, yeah.

MICHAEL. *(To* **MOM**.*)* So this is real?

MOM. Oh, yeah. The farm and the oil are real. Everything else, not so much.

UNCLE BOB. *(To* **GRANDMA**.*)* You're like a real live Beverly Hillbilly.

GRANDMA. *(Shoots him a look.)* Say, what?!

UNCLE BOB. I mean, you're not like that at all.

CARL. So "O-W 5" means…

GRANDMA. Oil well number five.

CARL. You're giving each of us an oil well?

GRANDMA. Yeah, why did ya want a sweater?

CARL, MICHAEL & STACY. No, no!

GRANDMA. 'Cause I can exchange the oil well for a sweater.

CARL, MICHAEL & STACY. No, oil well is good, I'll take the well, I'm happy with the oil well. *(Etc.)*

UNCLE BOB. You know, oil is not worth as much right now –

MICHAEL. Shut up, Bob, we're keepin' the wells!

JILL. *(To* **MICHAEL**.*)* Hey, you can buy back the plates!

STACY. Isn't that why you left him?

JILL. Uh-huh.

(Realizing.)

Oh, yeah.

GRANDMA. I mean, you've all proven that you can take my crap and that you're responsible and make relatively good decisions and won't squander the money, right, Michael?

MICHAEL. Absolutely.

GRANDMA. Because if ya do, I will take the wells back.

MICHAEL. Got it.

CARL. Have you been testing us today, Grandma?

GRANDMA. Of course. I don't act like a jackass all the time.

MOM. Well...

GRANDMA. I'm just tryin' to toughen you up, for your own good. Because a lot of people are gonna test you and throw stuff at you for the rest of your life, and you gotta be strong and not let it affect you, or you're gonna get squashed like a bug.

STACY. This is unbelievably nice of you, Grandma. I mean, this is a life changer.

MICHAEL & CARL. Oh yeah, really nice, life changer, thank you, incredible, unbelievable. *(Etc.)*

GRANDMA. You're welcome. Now don't screw it up.

UNCLE BOB. Do I get an oil well?

GRANDMA. What is this, Christmas?

UNCLE BOB. Dangit. What about Helen?

GRANDMA. Don't worry about Helen. I'm gettin' her a house. We need to get outta this dump.

MOM. "We"?

GRANDMA. I'm gonna take care of you, hon. We'll get matching tattoos.

MOM. No, we won't.

GRANDMA. It's you and me, kid. If you think I'm gonna outlive you, you got another thing comin'.

MOM. Is this negotiable?

GRANDMA. No. Look, I know I've never said this, but I just want you to know how special you've always been to me. You are the light of my life. You grew up to be such a wonderful, loving person in spite of how I raised you. You're so brave and strong, and I'm so proud of you. And you've got three wonderful kids… Well, two anyway.

(CARL *and* STACY *both point to* MICHAEL.)

MICHAEL. I'm not *that* bad!

CARL, STACY & JILL. Well…

GRANDMA. *(To* MOM.*)* I love you, honey, and I'll always be there for ya.

STACY. Did she just say the "L" word?

GRANDMA. New tradition.

MOM. I love you, too, Mom.

GRANDMA. *(To* STACY, CARL, *and* MICHAEL.*)* And I love you, Stacy, and I love you, Carl, and I love you, Michael,

(*To* JILL.*)*

And I even love you, umm…

JILL. Oh, it's –

GRANDMA. *(Smiling, tender.)* Jill. I know your name, honey.

STACY. And we love you, too, Grandma.

JILL. Yes, we do.

STACY. *(After a few beats, she looks at* MICHAEL *and* CARL.*)* Don't we.

MICHAEL & CARL. Oh, yeah, we sure do, oh, boy, do we, lots of love, love love love, and how. *(Etc.)*

GRANDMA. Okay, enough of the love-fest. Who won the grand prize?

STACY. I just wanna say one more thing.

GRANDMA. *(Groans.)* Ohh.

STACY. Carl, call your boss and tell him you'll do the article. You can write about me.

MOM. That's very nice, Stacy. You're in the lead.

GRANDMA. What?!

MICHAEL. *(Looks at* JILL *for approval.)* Yeah, go ahead, Carl. You can write about us, too.

MOM. Me, too.

UNCLE BOB. Me, too. What article?

GRANDMA. Can you put my phone number in it?

CARL. Thanks, everyone, but I'm not writing the article.

MOM. Why?

CARL. Because I don't wanna share my family with anyone.

JILL. *(How sweet.)* Ohh.

MOM. That's it. Carl wins.

GRANDMA. What?!

MOM. And the grand prize is…the honeymoon suite on the cruise.

CARL. *(Unsure if he likes the prize.)* Honeymoon suite?

GRANDMA. I gave away oils wells! This contest was rigged.

MOM. You'll get over it.

GRANDMA. Can we eat now, before Santa and his sleigh get here?

UNCLE BOB. That's not a sleigh. That's a government drone.

JILL.

WE WISH YOU A MERRY CHRISTMAS,

EVERYONE.

WE WISH YOU A MERRY CHRISTMAS,

WE WISH YOU A MERRY CHRISTMAS…

GRANDMA. I played Dorothy in *The Wizard of Oz*!

EVERYONE.

AND A HAPPY NEW YEAR.

(Blackout.)

End of Play

PROP AND COSTUME LIST

ACT I

Onstage Furniture:
1 dinner table, with table cloth
4 to 6 dinner table chairs
1 bar with various wine, beer, and liquor bottles behind/on it
2 bar stools
1 coffee table
1 sofa
1 easy chair
1 China cabinet
Christmas tree, decorated
3 Christmas ornaments in a box under the tree
Other various Christmas ornaments under the tree
Family photos
Christmas cards on display
Presents under the tree
Various Christmas decorations
Coat hooks on wall, or coat rack
Telephone

Carl brings in:
Winter coat
Laptop computer in a computer bag
Pen and notepad
Cell phone

Michael brings in:
Winter coat
Christmas card for Jill

Stacy brings in:
Winter coat
Bottle of wine
Cell phone
Purse

Uncle Bob brings in:
Winter coat
Bottle of whiskey
Cell phone
Beef jerky

Jill brings in:
Winter coat
Purse

Tote bag containing a small gift bag of cookies, and a present for
Michael containing the *Star Trek* Captain Series commemorative plate

Other Props:
Tray of little wiener appetizers (Mom)
Cheese ball and crackers (Stacy)
Plate of Rice Krispies bars (set on the dining table)
Christmas cookies (set on the dining table)
Wine glass (Stacy)
7 Plates/silverware rolled up in cloth napkins/water glasses (Mom)
Bottles of beer (Carl)
Bottle of Scotch (Uncle Bob)
Glass of water (Mom)
Santa hat (Uncle Bob)
2 Mistletoes, one to pin to the Santa hat (Uncle Bob)
Salt & Pepper shakers (Grandma)

ACT II

Other Props:
3 Christmas cards for the kids (Grandma)

COSTUME PLOT:

Carl
Casual or Khaki Pants
Nice shirt or sweater

Mom
Christmassy dress, and possible apron

Grandma
Christmasy dress

Michael
Sport coat
Slacks
Bow tie

Stacy
Casual pants and top

Jill
Pretty dress

Uncle Bob
Casual or khaki pants
Christmas sweater, the kind Uncle Bob would wear

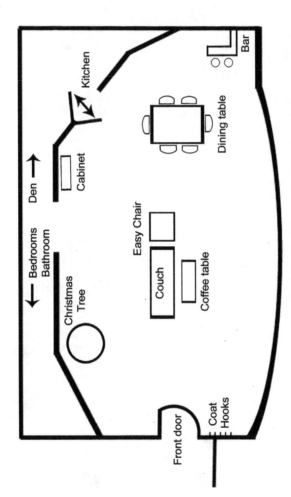

Kitchen

Den →

← Bedrooms
Bathroom

Cabinet

Christmas
Tree

Easy Chair

Couch

Coffee table

Dining table

Bar

Front door

Coat
Hooks

A Nice Family Christmas Set Design

Printed in the USA
CPSIA information can be obtained
at www.ICGtesting.com
LVHW011259230923
758932LV00012B/1034

9 780573 705236